THE GIRL WITH STARS IN HER HAIR

ALEXES RAZEVICH

CONTENTS

PROLOGUE

**Hermosa Beach, California
January 1919**

Father had thrown off the covers again. His face and what I could see of his body outside his wet pajamas were slick with sweat and nearly as white as the sheet that was tangled with the discarded blankets. Only his lips were dry, swollen and cracked from the fever. His breath came in hard, wheezing gasps. Mother adjusted the white cotton facemask tied over her mouth and nose, then dipped the cotton washrag into the basin of cold water on the nightstand next to the bed. She wrung it out and laid it across his burning forehead.

It seemed wrong for Father to be so sick in a room this cheerful—walls the clear blue of a summer sky, red-and-blue Turkish rug on the floor, cherry wood four-poster bed, paintings of the sea and ships on every wall—but sick he was.

Spanish flu. Father had caught it months after coming home from the Great War in Europe. Stupid to survive a war only to come home and die from influenza. Mother and I had been lucky so far—in the months the flu had been killing people all over the world, neither of us had suffered from so much as the sniffles. Every day the newspaper printed the death toll—numbers so high I couldn't make sense of them. School had been suspended for fear of spreading the disease, but not before seven of my classmates and my favorite teacher from the fourth grade had been struck down. Now my best friend, Moira, was sick with it. And Father. Father was as sick as I'd ever seen someone be, his lips a terrible shade of blue. I couldn't bear to think we might lose him.

"You shouldn't be in here," I said to Mother through the cotton facemask I wore.

She nodded, but continued sitting in the straight-backed wooden chair by the narrow bed, holding Father's hand as if she could will him back to health with her touch.

"You have to think about the baby," I said.

Mother had just that morning told me she was pregnant, but it'd been obvious for a while now. I was excited about finally having a little brother or sister but was old enough to know that if she got sick, it could harm the little being growing inside her. Over the years, she'd lost three babies before they were born—a girl, a boy, and one too early to know what it would have been.

She'd told Father the good news today as well, but he'd only shivered in his fever and moaned, not understanding her words. Mother's eyes had filled up with tears, but she'd quickly wiped them away, swept a few stray hairs—the same chestnut color as mine—back from her face, and got on with her nursing.

Down the hall, our Irish setter, Molly, started barking crazily. She only barked like that at strangers, and I couldn't imagine who could be approaching—not with the big red quarantine signs nailed to the front door and placed in every window that faced the Strand or the empty lots on each side of our house.

Not that many people were at the beach this time of year anyway. Only something like three or four thousand people lived in Hermosa Beach year round, and with the flu raging most were staying indoors as much as possible. We wouldn't be at the beach house now ourselves, normally. We came only in the summer, but Mother had brought us here now, in November, thinking the sea air would help Father recover faster.

She started to rise, but I said, "I'll go," and headed for the door, pulling down my face mask and saying, "Hush, Molly. Hush." But Molly wouldn't. She kept jumping toward the door, barking and snarling, her red hackles sticking up high.

Through the milk-glass panes of the front door I saw a man standing patiently on our wide wooden porch, seemingly oblivious to the dog barking furiously on the other side. I grabbed Molly by the collar and made her go into the parlor. I shut the door on her but her barking didn't subside. She couldn't see the man anymore, but I suppose she could smell him or maybe she'd just worked herself into such a tizzy that she couldn't shut it down. All that barking was bound to upset Mother and likely Father too, since it seemed loud enough to penetrate even the deepest delirium.

I opened the front door a crack and peeked out. Looking past the man, I saw that no one was out on the Strand on this chilly winter day, and the beach immediately beyond was deserted. A cold wind blew past me, and I shivered.

The man waiting on the porch was the most average person I'd ever seen: average height and weight, mouse-brown hair cut short, and a clean-shaven, ordinary face. He wore a good wool suit and vest, and a gray felt hat. He carried a small black-leather satchel. The only outstanding things about him were his eyes. They were the shocking clear blue of the Pacific Ocean on the best of days.

"Excuse me one moment, please," I said through the crack and shut the door.

"Where are your manners?" I said sharply to Molly and grabbed her collar again. She didn't want to go, but I hauled her down the hall and through the kitchen at the rear of the house to the back door. I opened the door with one hand and pushed Molly into the fenced back yard with the other. Even then her barking didn't subside.

I opened the door fully and waited for the man to state the reason for his visit.

"Good morning," he said and politely doffed his hat. "I am Dr. Gremhahn. I've been told that your father is ill. I can cure him."

"That's a very bold statement," I said, glancing at his satchel. It was much smaller than the one Father carried to see his patients.

He quirked his head but kept his expression serious. "You are quite bold yourself, for a girl of—?"

"Fourteen," I said.

He raised his eyebrows a touch at my answer but said, "Is your mother at home? I'd like to speak with her."

I left him standing on the porch and started back toward Father's room. Before I got halfway there, the door opened and Mother came out, wiping her hands on the white apron with ruffles all around that she wore over her dark-blue housedress. Her facemask, like mine, now dangled around her throat.

"There's a man at the door who says he can cure Papa," I said, keeping my voice low.

Mother's eyes widened but she said only, "I'll speak with him. Go sit with your father, please."

Father was covered in sweat again when I sat down next

to his bed. He must have been dreaming about something horrible, because he moaned and rolled back and forth in his sleep. I took his hand in mine. It was thin and boney, not like the strong hands I remembered from before he went to the war and came home, only to get sick. He never should have gone—he was too old—but they were desperate for doctors over there and he never could leave anyone to suffer. I pulled the washrag from the water, wrung it out and laid it on his forehead. This seemed to soothe him, and he was resting easier by the time Mother and the gentleman entered the room.

The gentleman was either confident or crazy, since he wore no covering over his nose and mouth. Mother had pulled her facemask up over the bottom half of her face, as had I.

"Thank you, Cassie," Mother said, dismissing me.

I went to the door, opened and closed it, then squeezed myself up tight against the wall so I could watch. Mother and the doctor were much too focused on Father to notice me there.

The doctor felt Father's forehead with the back of his hand and then held his wrist to take his pulse. He bent over close to Father's face and inhaled a great breath of Father's raspy exhalation, drawing it into himself, then twisted his head a little, the way someone might when trying to make sense of something he'd just learned.

He straightened up, nodded once, and reached into his bag, drawing out a glass bottle filled with a golden liquid. He carefully removed the stopper and dribbled a few drops on Father's chest, all the while muttering words I couldn't understand but didn't think were English. He sprinkled more drops up and down Father's fevered body, taking care to spill several drops on Father's wrists and ankles.

The doctor stood and I thought he was done. But it

seemed he wasn't, because he leaned over Father again, putting his ear up near Father's mouth this time, and cupped his hand the way people do when they are trying to hear something faint.

Mother kept her eyes on him as if he were both the most fascinating and most worrisome thing she'd ever seen. I thought that if the gentleman made a wrong move, Mother might bean him with the washbasin.

He took another small flask from his bag—this one silver, a small version of the type in which some men kept alcohol. I saw Mother stiffen when she glimpsed it, but she didn't put out a hand to stay the gentleman nor say anything to him. I watched as the doctor upended the silver flask, poured some clear liquid onto his fingers and then ran those fingers over Father's forehead, making little wavy lines on his skin. The doctor poured a small amount on a spot between Father's eyebrows just above his nose, and, finally, some on his mouth.

Father sighed and licked his parched lips, his tongue gathering the drops and taking them in. The doctor sat still, watching Father, waiting for something I thought, then nodded as though satisfied.

"Change those sheets," the doctor said, and he rose and strode from the room. "And open those windows."

Mother shot me a harsh look when she spied me standing against the wall, but all she said as she followed the man out was, "Will you have some tea?"

"Thank you," the doctor said. "It will sweeten the discussion of payment."

Oh, here it comes, I thought, but thought too that this doctor didn't know my mother. She would never fall for some snake-oil charlatan's demand for high payment. She might give him a dollar or two, but no more, I was sure of that. If he insisted, she might give him a slap upside the head before sending him on his way.

"Of course," the doctor said, "nothing is due until I have proven my worth by restoring your husband to full health."

I settled in the chair next to Father's bed and laid the back of my hand on his forehead, just as I'd seen the doctor do. It seemed to me he wasn't as burning hot as he'd been before, and his lips were less blue.

In the morning, just as the doctor had promised, Father was up and around as if he'd never been sick at all. But there was something different about him—a thing I couldn't put a name to. Something *not right*.

ONE

Hermosa Beach, California
June 1923

Father had gone into town to see his patients. He seemed to do this more now than in years past, and to stay later and later, often not getting home to the beach house until after I was asleep and leaving again right after breakfast. Mother had gone up to Morse and Morse, the grocers, leaving me to watch baby James. It would have been an easier job had he still been a baby, but he was a mad, tousle-haired boy in the Fearsome Fours. Chasing after him around the house, stopping him from pulling poor old Molly's tail, or yanking the tablecloth, rattling the dishes set out for dinner, and causing the candlesticks to fall over was exhausting. Tablecloth-yanking was his latest invention, and it seem to please him beyond measure to watch me dive to catch whatever was about to hit the floor. He never did it around Mother or Father. He saved this trick for when it was just the two of us. Brat.

I scooped him up in my arms. "Come on, Jimmy. Let's go

outside for a bit." He squirmed and kicked, but it was only for form. He loved being outside, seeing the people strolling up and down the Strand and out on the beach. He loved digging in the sand, gathering shells, and running along the waterline. I think he loved the beach nearly as much as I did.

There were plenty of people out today—finally summer and the sun like a big egg yolk in the blue-blue sky. Large beach umbrellas in various colors, set so close together they overlapped one another, covered the narrow stretch of sand between the Strand and the water. I glanced up Santa Fe Avenue as we passed by and saw it was stuffed full of cars. People came from as far away as Pasadena and the San Fernando Valley to enjoy the cooling air at the shore. Men and boys in short pants and women in short-sleeved or even sleeveless bathing costumes happily strolled the narrow Strand, crowded the beach, or played in the gentle surf. The smell of salt mixed with the tangy aroma of hot dogs and sauerkraut or pretzels from the vendor's rolling carts filled the air.

We'd been here a week already and would stay until the end of August. My friend Moira, who'd survived the flu, was coming in two days to stay with us until we went back to the big house in Los Angeles. I could hardly wait. I preferred the beach house over the big house—loved the coziness of it and the nearness of the sea—but I missed my friends while we were here.

Jimmy might have been only four, but he weighed thirty-five pounds. My arms were beginning to ache from carrying him, but I knew that the moment I set him down he'd scoot away. We'd passed the Berth Hotel at Tenth and the Strand, a six-block walk from our house, and were coming up on the bowling alley when I just couldn't carry him anymore.

"I'm going to put you down," I said. "Don't run off. Take my hand, okay? We'll go down under the pier."

Jimmy nodded solemnly, but I saw mischief in his eyes.

The moment I set him down he bolted toward the water. I chased after him, calling his name, and caught him by the arm before he'd gotten too far.

Another hand had seized Jimmy's other arm, and I looked up. It'd been more than four years and I'd seen him only that one time, but I knew him in an instant—the doctor who'd saved my father.

"Hello," he said, letting go of Jimmy's arm and ruffling my brother's hair. "Do you remember me?"

"Yes, Sir," I said. He was wearing a different suit, every bit as fine and well cut as the one he'd worn the day he came to our house, but out of place among the beachgoers.

He nodded as if rewarding me for having given the right answer. "Are your parents at home?"

"Not at the moment, Sir," I said, "but they should be home shortly."

He nodded again, then crouched down to Jimmy's level and smiled at him, his eyes scanning Jimmy's face as though seeking something specific.

"This is my brother, James," I said. "He wasn't born when you came to help my father."

The doctor looked up. "Oh, I know who this is. I've been looking forward to meeting him."

A chill ran through me—odd on such a hot day. Had the gentleman spied on us? Jimmy, being Jimmy, was tugging at my arm, wanting to go to the water, even as the gentleman seemed to be memorizing my brother's face. I half expected him to suddenly turn out to be a gypsy and pronounce on Jimmy's future.

"If you'll excuse us," I said. "Shall I tell my parents we saw you?"

He stood up and said, "Yes, thank you. Tell them I will be by tonight. There's still the matter of payment due."

I turned and watched as he strode away, Jimmy pulling my arm the other direction, toward the water. It wasn't like Mother or Father to not pay a bill when first presented. Maybe the doctor had never presented his bill. That was possible.

"Come on," Jimmy whined, yanking at my arm with all his four-year-old strength. I gave in and we walked down to the shore.

~

*M*other's scream tore me from a sound sleep. Thin morning light filtered through the pull-down shade and lace curtains in my bedroom. I glanced at the clock on the dresser: 6:25. I threw off the sheet and ran barefoot toward Father's bedroom, thinking something must have happened to him, that he fell or was sick again, something horrible to make Mother shriek like that. I realized her scream had come from the nursery just as Father threw open his door and raced down the hall toward that room, with me right on his heels.

Mother stood by Jimmy's little bed, her mouth open, sucking in noisy breaths. Her eyes were open wide but she was blinking, too, over and over. Father shouldered her aside a bit and they both stood and stared at the bed, blocking my view. They stood as still as stones.

Dead. Jimmy must be dead. Babies died unexpectedly often enough that everyone knew a family it had happened to. Tears sprang to my eyes. I crept up and peeked.

The bed was empty.

"Papa? Mama?"

They seemed to spring back to wakefulness at my words.

"Call the police," Mother said, but Father was already halfway across the room before she'd even spoken, heading for the kitchen butler's pantry, where we kept our telephone.

I slipped my hand into Mother's and asked in a small voice, so as not to make her more upset than she already was, "What happened? Where's Jimmy?"

Her voice, usually so calm and sure, shook when she spoke. "I don't know, honey. I don't know."

I looked at the window on the wall across from Jimmy's crib. It was shut, as always. No matter how hot it got at night, Mother and Father always made sure all the windows were shut and the doors locked, especially at the beach house. Summer at the beach meant strangers around, not like at home in the city where we knew all our neighbors and looked out for one another. I couldn't fathom why a burglar would steal a toddler.

The police came—three of them in their long blue coats with silver buttons down the front, a sheen of sweat on all their faces, as the day was already warm. They asked a lot of questions and dumped black powder all over all the windowsills and doorknobs and said they'd be in touch as soon as they knew anything. They told Father to phone Detective O'Malley when we got a call or letter asking for ransom.

I didn't know how they could be so sure a ransom demand would come, but they seemed confident it was just a matter of time—more likely hours than days. Mother and Father seemed to think the same.

They pulled up two chairs next to the telephone and waited. Mother was beside herself with worry, her arms pulled tight against her body and her face tense. Father looked ready to kill, his fist balled and his face red. He stared at the telephone, all the while tapping his left heel hard against the floor. I thought I would almost pity the kidnappers if my father got to them before the police.

I sat on the floor away from them, my back against the wall, and wondered if I should have told the police about seeing Dr. Gremhahn on the beach yesterday and how the way he'd looked at Jimmy had made my stomach churn.

Hours passed. No call came and no letter was received. Father took to pacing in the kitchen. Mother refused to leave her chair. The sun had long set, and my hunger could no longer be quelled with water.

I went to the icebox and took out a roasted chicken. Mother and Father glanced at me. I'm sure they were hungry, too, but Mother turned back to staring at the telephone and Father kept right on pacing and muttering under his breath. I took a loaf from the breadbox and cut six slices. I carved the chicken and made a sandwich for each of us, put them on plates and set them all on the table. I poured three glasses of cold tea and set them beside the plates, then sat down and started eating. Father grabbed his sandwich off the plate and tore at it like an animal while he paced. Mother said, "Thank you, Cassie," but didn't touch the food.

"Mama, you should eat something," I said. "'All sorrows are less with bread,' you always say."

She almost smiled and said, "Cervantes."

I nodded. "Eat a little at least. Please."

Her gaze moved to the plate. She picked up the sandwich and nibbled. It was something, at least.

$\sim$

*D*ays went by. Moira didn't come to stay after all. Father went back to work, driving just after sunup from the beach to the hospital downtown and driving back at night, usually so late that Mother and I were both long gone to bed by the time he returned. This had been going on since right after Father's cure and didn't surprise me anymore, but it didn't make me miss him any less.

Outside, summer beach life went on. We heard hordes of laughing children, saw smiling families laden down with beach umbrellas and towels, watched teenagers walking arm in arm, girls giggling as they passed stands of boys in bathing costumes. Mother and I sat in the house day after day.

"What a lovely day," she'd exclaim to me almost every morning. "Why don't you change into your bathing clothes and take a swim?"

And almost every morning I'd look out the window and say, "I don't really feel like a swim today. Maybe tomorrow."

"How about a stroll then?" she'd say. "Maybe at the water's edge? It'll be cooler there than in the house."

I'd act like she hadn't made that exact suggestion a dozen times already and say, "I'll go if you come with me."

She'd clench her jaw, look at the phone that rarely rang, then glance nervously toward the front door that she'd run to twice a day when the post arrived, desperate for the ransom note that never came.

If I went to the beach and swam, who would make her a cup of tea when her heart fell yet again? If it weren't for Molly needing her twice-daily walk and our weekly forays to Morse and Morse for food, it's likely neither of us would have ever left the cottage.

At least she had a more comfortable chair now. I'd moved out the hardback one she'd sat in the day the police came and pulled in a club chair from the front parlor. She'd smiled and thanked me. It was good, I thought, that she'd noticed. Good that she'd smiled. Most of the time her body was tight with tension and her eyes hooded with that look of someone lost inside their own mind, her thoughts a dire maelstrom.

"Mama," I said one morning a month after Jimmy had

disappeared, "what about the finder woman? Maybe it's time to see her."

Mother shook her head. I knew she didn't believe in the finder woman's abilities, even though our neighbor down the way, Mrs. Jensen, swore the finder woman had known exactly where Mrs. Jensen's lost brooch had been and had named the place their dog was hiding when it had run away. Gypsies, psychics, and the like were not on Mother's list of people to consult or know.

"I think it's time for Molly's walk," she said, and rose like a somnambulist to get Molly's leash.

Weeks passed. Cabin fever set in, for me if not for Mother. I took to riding the Red Car to the downtown library every few days, just to get out. I spent one night with Moira, but felt guilty leaving Mother and declined my friend's next invitation.

I came home from the library one day and found mother dressed in her going-out clothes, her gloves and hat waiting on the mahogany hall-table by the front door. I was glad she was finally leaving the house.

Then my heartbeat sped up. Why was she going out? Had the ransom call finally come? I hadn't left the house in days and I go off for a few hours to get some books to read and the kidnappers choose that moment to make their demands?

"Where are you going?" I asked as I dropped my books next to her hat on the hall-table.

Mama touched my arm. Here eyes were bright and calm for the first time since Jimmy had vanished.

"I've decided you were right, Cassie. We're going to see the finder woman. We're going to bring Jimmy home."

TWO

Hermosa Beach, California
July 1923

The finder woman lived on First Street in a small house with a red door. The red door was how people found her. Dabbling with the occult was popular among a certain "smart" set these days, but not with people like us. The wife and daughter of a prominent Los Angeles physician would never go to someone like her—a teller of fortunes, finder of lost things, speaker with the dead. Mother and I probably wouldn't have gone, but our neighbor down the way, Mrs. Lou, had come by earlier in the week to bring us a loaf of brown bread she'd baked. She'd spoken to Mother about the finder woman, saying that the woman "wasn't a phony like those fake gypsies in Redondo Beach. She's not just after your money. She wants to help." Between Mrs. Jensen and Mrs. Lou, Mother had somehow been persuaded. Or she'd grown desperate enough in her heart to try anything.

Mrs. Lou had said to bring something of Jimmy's with us,

ALEXES RAZEVICH

and something of personal great value as a thank you for the help—so much for the finder woman not being after money. I'd peeked in Mother's handbag and seen Jimmy's favorite stuffed toy—a tiger—and one of the pearl-and-diamond rings she'd inherited from her mother. I couldn't believe Mother would even consider giving away something that valuable or that meaningful. I kept my mouth shut, though.

It was a good-weather day—neither hot nor cold and with the tiniest breeze blowing. We both wore visiting clothes, as if we were going to see friends—Mother in a white-lace, drop-waist dress, white stockings and shoes, white hat with red silk roses on the side, and white lace gloves. I wore almost the same outfit, except my dress was blue and my hat plain.

Mother had the taxi driver drop us at the top of the hill, which was past the finder woman's house. I supposed she was a little embarrassed about our errand and didn't want even a stranger knowing where we were really going.

The homes were sparse here, with nothing but sand dunes dotted with dry vegetation between them. After the taxi had gone, we walked down the hill to the house with the red door. Mother took in a great deep breath, marched up the steps and knocked firmly. I stood beside her, my throat dry and my stomach tingling. I'd never seen a magic person before. I wanted the woman to be truly magical—not a charlatan like Dr. Gremhahn, who I still didn't believe had actually cured Father. Lucky coincidence was all. I wanted the finder woman to be real and to bring Jimmy back to us. Mother knocked again.

The finder woman opened the door. I knew immediately she was the one, even though she didn't look the way I'd expected. She was older than me but younger than Mother, tall, with brown eyes and a round, kind face. Her dark hair was bobbed short, with bangs, like Bernice in Mr. Fitzger-

18

ald's story. She wore a green dotted Swiss dress, white stockings, and green shoes, and smiled as though we were expected—even though we weren't—and that she couldn't have been more pleased that we'd come.

She ushered us into a small but tidy parlor and invited us, with a nod, to sit on a plush yellow sofa with iron lion-claw feet. I don't know what I'd expected, but this very ordinary-looking woman in a house that any of my friends might have lived in wasn't it. It seemed there should be gauzy curtains wafting in an unfelt breeze and mystical signs on the walls, a crystal ball on a side table. Maybe a deck of tarot cards. At least a Ouija board.

Instead there was the yellow sofa, a lovely chaise covered in nubby white cotton, two straight-backed wooden chairs with green leather cushions, and a pair of walnut side tables. Each side table was topped with a brass lamp with a cut-glass shade. The fireplace mantel was festooned with what I assumed were family photographs. A large yellow-and-blue floral rug and a wrought-iron plant stand displaying a very healthy Boston fern completed the decor.

"Can I get you a cool drink?" the woman said.

Mother clutched her purse tight it in her lap and said, "No, thank you."

"I'm Diana Hasbro," the woman said, settling into one of the straight-backed chairs opposite the sofa where we were sitting. "You can give me your names or not, as you please."

It wasn't like Mother to be rude, but she didn't give our names in return. She squeezed the top of the purse she held and gazed at the finder woman as if in a trance. Maybe Mother was thinking this hadn't been a good idea after all.

I wiped my hands against my skirt thinking we should get out of here before something bad happened. This house and Diana Hasbro may have looked ordinary enough, but there was a something about them I couldn't put into words, a feeling that they were not what they appeared to be.

Diana smiled as if it were of no matter that Mother wouldn't give our names.

"How can I help you?" she said.

Mother blinked as if startled. She opened her handbag, reached inside, and drew out Jimmy's tiger. She gazed at it a moment, then handed it to the woman.

Diana reached for it. She didn't ask any questions, just clutched the stuffed toy to her chest. Her eyes filled with tears.

"I'm very sorry," she said softly.

I jumped up from the sofa and yelled, "No! Jimmy's not dead. He can't be dead."

I looked at Mother. Her face was ashen. She'd thrown her hand over her mouth, as if to stifle a scream. I could see she'd contemplated many times that Jimmy might not be living, but the shock of my saying it out loud had nearly undone her. I sat down quickly and took her hand in mine.

"Your son isn't dead," Diana said to Mother.

Relief blasted through me, and then my cheeks grew hot. I'd spit out my worst fear and upset my mother—which I'd never meant to do.

Diana went on as if I'd not said a word.

"Your son is alive. I feel his life force still in this world, but it's very strange." The finder woman pressed the tiger tighter to her chest, then asked, "Do you have anything else of him with you?"

Mother swallowed deeply and nodded. She went into her handbag again and drew out a small brown-and-white cowry shell. "I found this in his room after he—after he disappeared. I think somehow it's connected."

Diana put out her hand and flinched slightly when Mother put the shell in her palm. The woman looked at the thing a long moment before closing her fingers around it and shutting her eyes.

"Gremhahn," she said, her eyes still closed.

I heard Mother's quick intake of breath and felt own my pulse race. Dr. Gremhahn was the man who'd supposedly cured Father. How could the finder woman know about him at all, much less know his name? Were they working together on some elaborate scheme, with my mother as their patsy?

Diana opened her eyes and handed the shell back to Mother.

"I'm very sorry," she said again.

Mother dropped the shell back in her handbag. She shut it with a resolute snap of the clasp.

"What has Dr. Gremhahn to do with my son's disappearance?"

A shiver ran across Diana's shoulders. "He's no doctor. A *gremhahn* is a sea dweller, a shape-shifting goblin thief who steals children."

Mother's eyes opened wide.

"But that's not what's happened here," Diana said quickly. She paused then, opening and closing her hands several times rapidly, as if trying to grab knowledge from the air. "The gremhahn has taken your son and kept him alive, but changed," she said.

"What do you mean, 'changed'?" Mother said. "Changed how?"

"I don't know. I can't *see* where he is. *What* he is. He feels different. Changed. I don't know the reason why."

"Payment," I whispered. "The doctor said he'd come that night for his payment."

Mother heard me and she stared in my direction, her eyes still wide but blind to the room in which she sat.

"Oh no, no, no," she muttered. "Did I save my husband at the price of my son?"

"*H*ave you lost your mind completely?" Father yelled.

He and Mother were downstairs in the kitchen. His voice was so loud it carried up to me as though we were in the same room. Molly lifted her head and growled lightly. I scratched behind her ears and made soothing noises to calm her. Then I did something terrible. I tiptoed to the window and opened it wider, the better to hear what they were arguing about.

Mother's voice was quieter than Father's, but I heard her say, "I can't stand the not knowing, Charles. I can't stand thinking I see him in every little blond boy on the beach, on the trolley, in the market. I had to find the truth."

"That a sea goblin had stolen our child?"

Father's voice was so mean it made me wince. He never used to yell. He used to be kindness itself. Mother had said that the war had changed him, but I was pretty sure she didn't really believe that. I was pretty sure we both knew it was losing Jimmy that had done it—that pain and guilt had taken away my kind father and Mother's loving husband.

Except that Father had changed before that, before Jimmy was even born. Maybe it was the illness that had done it; the flu had hurt his brain and hardened his heart. He was never the same after he recovered. Lately he'd grown so distant and cold, I didn't mind that he was hardly ever home.

If Mother answered him, I couldn't hear her words. But I heard Father yell, "Get away from me. You let that man into the house, that so-called doctor. If not for you, Jimmy never would have been kidnapped. I can't look at your face."

Molly raised her head and growled again, harder this time.

I held my breath, rubbing gently between Molly's shoulders. Usually that soothed her, but she jumped away from where we sat by the window and pawed at my closed door. I heard the kitchen door slam shut and hard, angry footsteps pound down the hall toward their bedroom.

Then the kitchen door slammed again and more footsteps sounded. It must have been the other one chasing whoever had left first. I heard the awful sound of flesh hitting flesh, heard Mother cry out, and then feet running and another door slam.

I walked to the door and sat on the floor beside Molly. My throat felt tight and as dry as beach sand, but my eyes were too open. I wanted to run to Mother and comfort her, but I knew her pride needed me to pretend I hadn't heard a thing. I cried into Molly's soft fur with tears that felt like they would never stop.

~

*W*hen Father packed up his clothes but told Mother to stay at the beach house I wasn't surprised. After last night, I thought they both felt too guilty to face the other—Father because he'd gone off to war when he didn't have to, only to come home and get sick. If it weren't for the flu, Dr. Gremhahn never would have come to our house. Mother because she blamed herself for letting the doctor in, even serving him tea. And Father had hit her. That was a thing neither could forgive.

Father came to my room and shut the door softly behind him.

"I think you know your mother and I won't be living together anymore," he said.

I swallowed hard and nodded.

He sat on the edge of my bed. "Would you like to come back with me? We can bring Molly, if you like."

My mouth was as dry as paper. My throat felt like rock was lodged inside. I was more than half afraid of the thing that lived in Father's skin now, and I couldn't leave Mother alone in her grief and misery. I was the one who took Jimmy to the beach that day. If Dr. Gremhahn was the kidnapper, then I was the one who'd showed him my brother.

"I think I'd like to stay here with Mother," I said softly, hardly able to make the words come out.

Father sighed, and the sadness in his eyes almost made me believe he was his own self again, almost changed my mind. Even if this had brought my real father back, it was Mother who needed me most.

~

That Sunday I went to church alone—Mother had said she wasn't feeling well. When I came into the house, I saw Mother's wide-brimmed sunhat, white gloves, pocketbook, and a largish carpetbag in the foyer. I stared at them, my stomach roiling with nerves—she seemed to have had a quick recovery from whatever had ailed her. I pulled off my own lace church gloves and removed my hat. Mother barely left the house anymore. Why were her traveling things out?

"Mama?" I called, because I couldn't see her in the parlor, dining room, or kitchen, though Molly looked up at me from beneath the kitchen table and thumped her tail three or four times.

"Hey, girl," I said to her softly. She was getting on in years. The days when she jumped up to greet me when I walked into the house were long gone.

Mother came out of her bedroom wearing white linen trousers with a long-sleeved seafoam-green blouse. Never, ever, had I seen my mother in pants.

"Close your mouth," she said. "A woman can wear trousers nowadays."

I made a show of clamping my lips together and ran my fingers across my lips as if zipping them shut. Mother laughed.

"I have a pair for you, too," she said, excitement in her voice. She disappeared back into her room and reappeared carrying a pair of tan trousers. She held them out to me as though they were encrusted with jewels.

I took them, asking, "What's this about?"

Mother crooked her finger. "Come sit in the parlor. I'll tell you."

A funny, nervous wiggle slithered through me. What could she have to say that was so strong I needed to be seated for it? Molly must have wondered, too, since she levered herself up and slowly followed us in. She flopped down on the floor by my feet and looked expectantly toward Mother.

When we were all settled, Mother drew in a deep breath, let it out, and said, "We're going to find the sea goblin and make him return Jimmy to us."

I stared at her, my mind stunned by the crazy statement. Mother didn't sound or look crazy, though. She sounded and looked the way she did when she'd made up her mind about something.

"How would we find the sea goblin?" I said cautiously.

She stood and drew a small gold compass from her pocket. "Diana, the finder woman, gave me this. It will point the way for us. If it points west, there's nothing we can do—the goblin is safe in his water home. But if it points north, south, or east, we can find him. Capture him. Force him to give Jimmy back."

First of all, I doubted the finder woman had *given* Mother the compass. More likely another piece of valuable jewelry had changed hands. Second, no compass could home in on an individual. Nothing but disappointment could come from this adventure. Third, Mother's voice was much too matter-of-fact for the statement she'd just made.

I opened my mouth to speak, but she cut me off with a wave of her hand.

"I know what you're thinking, but I've been testing the compass for three days now. I've stood in the backyard in the same spot each time and faced west. Sometimes the compass points west, but mostly it points south. South is the way we'll go." The fire of belief shone in her eyes. She nodded forcefully. "We will find the gremhahn, the sea goblin. We will get Jimmy back."

I knew my mother. She'd go without me if I raised an objection. I couldn't let her go alone.

"When are we leaving?"

Mother smiled; relieved, I thought. "Today. Go pack a bag. I've arranged care for Molly. We'd take her with us, but she's getting a bit long in the tooth for a journey that could last a day, a week, a month."

She said the times like they were all the same—a day, a month. Why not a year?

"How are we going? Papa took the car."

Mother pursed her lips and nodded—at the problem that had been in her mind, I supposed—and then smiled ruefully. "We'll be walking. Mostly on the shore, I assume. The sea is his home. Diana says he doesn't like to stray far from it."

Diana it was now—familiar, like a friend. While I was at the market or rode downtown to the big library, did Mother spend time with the finder woman?

And walking? For a week? A month?

"It's the only way, Cassie," she said. "I have the compass. We'll find Jimmy. We'll bring him home. That's all there is to it."

I knew Mother wasn't crazy, not in that lunatic asylum

way, but this—this was determination that stood very close to the edge. Determination that could only bring sorrow. All the more reason I had to go with her.

~

$\mathscr{M}$other took Molly, who probably thought she was going on a nice walk, to Mrs. Lou's while I packed a bag, trying to guess what I might need. I changed out of my church dress and into a white short-sleeved blouse, the tan trousers, and black-and-white saddle shoes, the most comfortable walking shoes I owned. All the while my mind spun with practical questions. How were we going to eat on this week, month, who-knew-how-long journey? Where would we sleep? If we were gone when Father came, what would he think? He'd worry. I hoped he'd worry. Had she called and told him, giving him the truth or some story that would be more comfortable for him to believe? What had Mother told Mrs. Lou about where we were going and why? I supposed I should ask Mother—get our lies straight.

I heard the front door open and close and Mother's quick steps coming up the stairs and then toward my bedroom.

She knocked twice and opened the door without waiting for me to answer.

"Are you ready?" she asked, her voice so light and cheerful that anyone else hearing her might think we were heading for a picnic.

Where does Papa think we're going? I wanted to ask. *You have told him, haven't you, so he won't come and find the house empty, frightening him to bits?* But I only picked up my bag, painted a smile I didn't feel on my face, and followed her down the hall toward the front door.

"It's a grand day for it," Mother said. "The weather is perfect for a walk." She put on her broad-brimmed sunhat and picked up her bag, then turned and looked at me over her shoulder. "We'll find that goblin in no time. A day, two, a week maybe, and we'll have Jimmy back."

"What if we don't?" I said as she opened the front door.

She stopped then, and her face grew serious. "I can't think that, Cassie. *We* can't think that. To even suppose we won't find the gremhahn, or that we will but not get Jimmy back—that we will fail—it is too much to bear."

I swallowed hard.

"Then we will," I said. "All of it—find the goblin, make him give Jimmy back."

Because I hoped that, even if there were no such thing as a sea goblin, if by some amazing turn of events we did get Jimmy back—that he could be gotten back—that it would bring Father back, too, and we would be a family again.

THREE

Hermosa Beach, California
August 1923

It was a good day for a stroll—the temperature cooler by the water. We trudged across the beach lugging our bags, past people stretched out on blankets in shorts or bathing costumes, down to where the tide packed the sand tight.

Half a dozen kids from a church group, to judge by the dress clothes left neatly folded on individual blankets, spotted us and came alongside, some hopping up and down, as if we were something out of an exciting sideshow.

"Where are you going, all dressed up?" asked a boy of about ten with neatly combed brown hair.

"Don't you have bathing costumes?" a red-haired, freckled girl asked in a worried voice, as if she thought us too poor for proper bathing attire.

I wanted to slide under the sand and hide. Mother, though, smiled and crouched to their level.

"We're on a quest," she told them, her voice mysterious and her eyes gleaming.

"What's a quest?" the brown-haired boy asked.

"It's a search," Mother said in her normal tone. "A search that could be long and hard but is important, so it must be done."

"What are you looking for?" the freckled girl asked.

Before Mother could answer, a woman in a black bathing costume ran up and shooed away the kids. I was glad for the interruption. I didn't want Mother to say we were looking for her son who'd been stolen by a sea goblin and we were on our way to get him back.

"I'm very sorry," said the woman who'd shooed off the kids. She wore black shoes tied with ribbons halfway up her calf. Her gaze slid up, down, and all over us, no different from the way the children's had.

"They were no bother," Mother said.

The woman turned to chase after her charges and we continued on.

∼

The farther south we went, the fewer people we saw, and I was glad for that.

I wasn't used to this much walking, and my legs were sore. My arms hurt from lugging the traveling bag that held my clothes, brush, comb, toothbrush, two pairs of shoes, two sets of white gloves, an evening hat, a Sunday dress and hat, and *Anna Christie*, the book I was reading. I certainly didn't need any more stares from the curious weighing me down.

Every twenty minutes or so Mother would take out the compass, face the ocean and check her bearings. She'd press her lips together and lead on.

We walked across Redondo Beach and then Torrance

Beach to the end, where it bordered the hills and cliffs of Palos Verdes. The sand gave out here, changing to rocks and boulders visible beneath the water's surface. Ahead, the hill rose up, presenting a sharp, unwelcoming cliff face. Mother frowned. She took out the compass and inhaled sharply.

"He's near, but not close," she almost whispered, even though there was no one around us to hear.

I shifted my gaze to the ocean and then back to the hill, a tan cliff that looked sliced by a knife, the brown and green vegetation, and the white boulders standing proud. "On land?"

Mother nodded. "Close to the sea but on land." She looked at the hill that stood between our quarry and us. "You always did like climbing."

Truth was, I was a tomboy when I was young and the love of adventure hadn't left me now that I was considered a young lady, old enough to marry. I could climb a hill nearly as easy as walking, but I wasn't sure Mother could make it. She was a strong swimmer, though, and I thought maybe we should swim around the point. But we'd either have to abandon our goods or get all we'd brought with us soaked. So, climbing it was—if Mother could make it.

But I'd let slip from my mind how determined she was. Resolve drove her up the hillside. She picked her way up a narrow, rutted path likely carved by rain, choosing her foot and handholds carefully, moving nearly as fast as I did.

Our reward for reaching the top was a flatish mesa, the land wild and studded with milkweed, sagebrush, and purple-blue-flowered phacelia. Mother took out the compass, drew in a deep breath and headed off at a quick pace along the cliff's edge. I followed her, glancing down at the sparkling blue ocean below, looking for a trail that would take us down again, but the cliff dropped straight into the boulder-dotted sea.

Finally I spotted a trail that looked as though it might lead down to the water. Mother had slowed her frantic pace by then, and we walked side by side. My legs were feeling the strain of so much unaccustomed walking. Words seemed too hard, so I touched her arm and pointed down.

She raised her eyebrows. I supposed she was growing a little too weary for words as well. Out came the compass again, Mother staring down at it, a tight smile forming on her lips.

"Closer now," she said.

"How can you know that?" I said, finding the strength for words.

She sighed lightly. "There's something I didn't tell you. This compass, it does more than tell what direction the gremhahn is traveling. It shows how close we are to him. It's in the colors."

She held the compass so I could see it, and I realized she had not done that before, not let me see what she saw on its face.

"See how the background is pale blue?"

I peered into the compass. The directions were in red. The needle was silver and pointed southwest. The background was a pale shade of robin's egg blue. I nodded to her.

"The closer we are to the gremhahn, the lighter the background becomes," she said. "When we set out this morning, the background was dark indigo. This light blue shows we're close."

We started down the narrow trail, following it even though we couldn't fully see where it would take us, knowing only that we were descending and that, hopefully, eventually we would reach water again. The ocean was calm, waves rolling gently toward a hidden shore. A dim sound like barking reached us and I could see dark shapes in the water.

We rounded a corner on the trail and a small crescent-shaped cove was revealed. Tall cliffs rose to the east and south. The barking was louder now, and I saw it came from maybe a dozen seals swimming in disjointed circles offshore. Usually seals were quiet, not like their noisy cousins, the sea lions, but these were clearly upset about something.

A man surf-fishing near the far end of the cove didn't turn to look when Mother and I came off the trail and onto the beach. The man was calm, lifting and dipping his pole as though all around him was perfect silence and peace.

I looked at Mother. She had the compass out again and I could see her eyes had widened even though she was looking down. I saw her jaw clench and her gaze shift over the fisherman as she slipped the compass back into her bag.

"Are you sure?" I asked.

She nodded. "The background is white. It's him."

"It's just a man," I said.

"No," Mother insisted. "It's the gremhahn. It's the evil goblin that stole our Jimmy. I know it."

"But he doesn't look like Dr. Gremhahn," I said.

"It doesn't matter. Remember, Diana said he could change his look. A shape-shifter, she said." Mother nodded forcefully. "It's him."

She seemed so sure, I almost believed her.

"And if we catch him?" I said.

"Diana gave me a binding spell," Mother said, as if that were the obvious answer. "And ways to make him talk."

I shaded my eyes and stared at the fisherman. He turned his head slowly and stared back. There was something in that stare, something cold, not human. And in that moment I believed my mother.

I ran.

Straight toward the fisherman, faster than Mother could run. Nothing mattered now, nothing but reaching the sea goblin first and bringing him down.

He saw me—he must have, since he kept looking right at me. He watched me, casually cranking in his line as I sped toward him. The rocky sand was wet; the bottom of my shoes made of smooth leather. I slipped on some seaweed, caught my balance, and ran. I heard Mother behind me, the slap of her shoes on the beach. The seals were going crazy, bobbing in the water and barking like an angry mob. I glanced over my shoulder at Mother. She was a distance behind me. I'd reach the goblin first.

My foot hit a hole. A sharp pang blasted across my ankle, and my right leg collapsed like a broken twig. I landed on my side on the wet sand, my breath knocked from my lungs.

In the few moments it took me to recover, a strange silence settled over the cove. Not a complete silence, just sounds that were gone—the raucous seals. I sat up and blinked. Seagulls wheeled overhead. The surf rolled in. The seals were gone. The goblin was gone.

Mother ran to me and crouched at my side. "Cassie! Are you all right?"

"I think so," I said. Mother took my arm and helped me stand. I took a deep breath, rolled my shoulders and shook out the leg I'd twisted. Everything seemed to work. Just to be safe I shifted my weight off the turned ankle.

"He knows we're after him now," I said.

Mother nodded. "I dare say he does. But perhaps he knew from the first moment. Perhaps he came to this deserted cove and showed himself on purpose. To demonstrate he knew we were coming. To show that he was a step ahead of us. To show that we would never capture him."

I thought the sea goblin didn't know my mother. If he had, he wouldn't have shown himself this way—it would only make her more determined.

She put her arm around me gently. "How's the leg?"

I shifted to try my weight on it, still nervous I might have seriously hurt myself. The ankle held.

"Fine. Let's keep going."

Mother took out her compass and frowned. "No point. He's gone west, into the sea. We might as well find a place to eat and sleep."

I looked at the nearly vertical hill between us and the dirt road that ran along the cliff edge. The only way up was back the long path we'd taken down. Mother and I sighed at the same moment and headed toward it.

At the top Mother stopped, looked me up and down and laughed.

"We look like a couple of hobos," she said.

I gave her the once-over back. "You certainly do. I'm sure I still look the fine-young-lady daughter of a prominent local physician."

I grimaced at my own words, worried that I'd upset Mother by mentioning Father. But she just laughed and ruffled my hair.

"That you do, Cassie. As beautiful in muddy trousers with sand in your hair as any debutante at a cotillion."

I rolled my eyes, but her words warmed me.

"Do we still head this way?" I said, taking a few steps.

"Yes," she said, checking the compass while walking alongside me. "He's back on land now and heading toward San Pedro."

"How far is that?" I was fading. Maybe saddle shoes hadn't been the best choice for a long walk.

"A ways," she said, "but at least we have a road to follow. I promise we'll rest once we get there."

"Good," I said. "I was afraid you'd want to walk all night, too."

She stopped and faced me. "I'm so sorry, Cassie. I've just been raging on in my own world. You're tired, aren't you?

You should be. I'm exhausted. Honestly, if we had camping gear I'd not go another step, but spend the night right here."

"Mother!" I cried in mock horror. "There could be mountain lions in these hills. Coyotes. Wouldn't you prefer a bed in a fine San Pedro hotel?" I gave her a sly smile. "Of course I am much younger, with more stamina. I could stay up all night to sit watch."

Mother laughed and we set off again with lighter hearts.

We hadn't gone far when a stake-bed truck with boxes piled high in the back pulled over and a Japanese man with two small children—both girls, their dark hair styled in two long braids—leaned over and said through the open rider's-side window, "Where're you heading? Maybe I give you a lift."

He didn't seem to think it at all odd that two women in dirt-smeared trousers carrying overnight bags were walking along the dirt road a long distance from anywhere. His girls stared at us goggle-eyed. They, at least, seemed to realize this was not a usual situation.

"San Pedro," Mother said, the slight rise in her voice at the end giving away the fact that we had no actual firm destination—not like *the Lighthouse Inn in San Pedro*, or *my cousin's house near the port*.

Or maybe the rise didn't mean that at all. Maybe it meant it really didn't matter where we went. Tomorrow we'd get up, Mother would consult her compass, and we'd be off whatever way it pointed.

"I can take you to downtown Sixth Street," the man said.

"That would be perfect," Mother said.

The man reached over and opened the passenger door.

"Get out, children," he said.

Mother shook her head. "We'll be fine in the back. Thank you."

It hit me when we settled in among the boxes of freshly

picked strawberries, their sweet scent filling our noses: exhaustion. Funny how that is—a person can go and go and even feel tired but still push on, but the moment one stops, fatigue comes crashing down. I could see a fresh tiredness had washed over Mother, too, but she sat up straight, her legs stretched out in front of her, her hands in her lap, as if riding in the back of a truck full of strawberries being driven by a total stranger was the most common thing in the world.

When we'd reached our nebulous destination and got out, Mother walked to his window and thanked him again.

"You best be careful on these beaches around here," he said. "Not everyone you meet by the sea will be someone you want to know." He paused. "Pay attention to the seals."

He drove away and I turned to Mother. "What do you suppose he meant by that?"

"I think," she said, "that he knows very well who—or what —the man surf-fishing was."

"And the seals?" I asked. "They didn't like the man on the beach."

"No," Mother said. "They didn't like him one bit."

FOUR

San Pedro, California
August 1923

We slept late—no surprise after our long walk of yesterday—and had a breakfast of eggs, toast, and coffee in a little café on Beacon Street. We'd washed our dirty trousers the night before—the bathtub water had turned brown-yellow with dirt, dust, and sand. This morning, with each of us in a fresh white blouse and summer gloves, we looked as neat and presentable as any mother-daughter duo out for a meal—if a tad eccentric in our clothing tastes.

While we waited for our change, Mother took out the compass and consulted it for the first time that day.

"He's gone south," she said, peering into the instrument, "but seems to have stopped now."

"Waiting for us?" I asked. "Like yesterday."

Mother glanced away—a thing she did when she was considering something. "Perhaps. Our hunt for him may be a game, in his view."

"But if he's always a step or more ahead . . ."

"Yes," she said. "Leading us on a merry chase."

A waiter brought our change and Mother distractedly stowed it in the steel-mesh coin purse Father had put in her stocking last Christmas. Father had excellent taste and the purse was beautiful, with glass-bead peacock feathers embroidered into the mesh. I wondered how Mother felt about it now, what she thought each time she brought it out.

I drew in a deep breath. "Can you see where the goblin has stopped?"

"No. Just that it's not close and he's still moving toward Mexico."

Mexico! That was more than one hundred miles away. Were we going to walk all the way to another country?

But then I thought, no, Mother just means in that direction. Even if we did have to go all that way, the gremhahn seemed to enjoy taunting us, and I doubted he would move faster than we could walk.

I picked up my bags and stood. "Then we'd best get started."

Mother grabbed her bags and stood as well. She looked at me a moment, then said, "Thank you, Cassie."

I shrugged to show that she needn't thank me. I had a whole list of my own reasons for joining Mother on this quest—seeing her happy again, having my brother back, maybe having a whole family, including Father, again. I'd walk barefoot from here to New York if it would make those things happen.

Mother brightened. "At least we can take a road today, until we get closer to him. Less wear and tear on us."

Small favors, I thought, and followed her as we headed toward the road that curved along the shoreline.

We'd trudged for maybe an hour or so, hardly talking. Now and then a car passed by, but no one stopped. The quiet and the thoughts chasing around in my mind were driving me crazy. If I hadn't fallen on the beach, would I have caught the gremhahn, or would he have poofed away in a cloud of smoke and laughter when I'd gotten close?

"Mama," I said, "will you teach me the spell?"

She startled out of whatever thoughts had consumed her. "Spell?"

"The binding spell. Will you teach it to me?"

Mother stopped and glanced away. I held my breath a little, waiting.

"That's a good idea." She cradled her carpetbag against her chest, opened it, and drew out a slip of paper. "Diana said I should memorize this, but somehow, each time I try, the words won't stay in my head. Maybe you'll do better."

I looked at the paper she handed me. There were two lines of writing—the upper in a language I didn't recognize, though I'd studied Latin and Greek. Written right below was what I assumed was a phonetic spelling of each undecipherable word.

"Do you have to pronounce everything perfectly?" I asked.

Mother nodded. "And in order."

"How do you say this first word, with a d j sound?"

"D'juan tee." Mother said. "Diana made me say it over and over until I got it right."

"D'jaun tee," I repeated. "D'juan tee, D'juan tee." I licked my lips. "And the next one?"

Mother looked down at the paper I'd angled so we could both see it, then back up quickly. She spun to face west. She'd heard it, the same as I had—like wings flapping, but there were no birds in sight.

"The second word." Mother stopped again. A dark gray fog rolled in so quickly we hadn't seen it coming, as if a thick, wet cloud had simply dropped from the sky on top of

41

us. Within moments the paper in Mother's hand grew moist and limp.

"Put it away," I said as I pushed the paper into her hand, afraid the fog would make the ink run and we'd lose the words. Even as I spoke, Mother was opening her carpetbag and tucking the paper safely inside. The fog was growing thicker. I shivered in the wet cold. Mother and I were close enough to reach out and touch, yet I could barely see her.

The sound of flapping wings started again, louder than before, coming from the northeast this time.

A large white-and-gray seagull dove through the fog, swooping past Mother's face. She made a guttural sound and batted the bird away with her hands. I batted at it, too, and it flew off.

"Cassie!" Mother called.

"Right here," I said. Trying to peer through the fog. "Are you all right?"

The fog rolled on, lifting enough that I could see her. Her eyes were wide and she clutched her carpetbag close to her body.

"Yes," she said, just as another gull—or maybe the same one—dove at her. A second seabird dove at me. And then another. And another. Birds came from all directions, beaks, claws, and wings slapping against us. Mother and I both ducked down and covered our faces with crossed arms.

The birds kept coming, cawing loudly, beaks open, their wings and clawed feet striking my shoulders, head, arms. I couldn't count how many there were. Dozens maybe. A whirlwind of feathered beasts swirling around us, screaming their gull calls, beating their wings and bodies against us.

And then, suddenly, the sound of a car horn blasting a long alarm. I didn't look up, but heard wheels rattling the gravel on the side of the road, then a door slamming shut and feet on the road and a man yelling, "Shoo. Shoo, and be gone. Go back where you came from, you wretches."

The gulls still swirled around us, but fewer now, and then none at all. They were gone. The fog had gone with them.

"You ladies all right?" a man's voice said. His voice had the slightest southern drawl.

I peeked up and saw the side of a shiny black Buick and two legs in blue jeans and brown cowboy boots.

Mother and I straightened up at the same moment. My eyes widened.

"Yes, now we are," Mother said, dusting herself off and picking up her carpetbag, which she'd dropped when the birds attacked the last time. "Thank you."

The man smiled—a flash of white teeth in the darkest brown face I'd ever seen. The tall gentleman held a straw cowboy hat in his hands that I thought he had probably used to shoo away the birds.

"Well, that's good," he said, returning the hat to his head and holding out a hand to Mother. "John Hayden."

Mother shook his hand. "Audrey Goodlight. And this is my daughter, Cassie."

"Pleased to meet you both," he said, as if we'd just been introduced over tea and cookies at church. "Can I offer you a ride somewhere?"

Mother peered at him much the same way she peered into the compass and said, "We'd be very grateful for the favor of a ride to Long Beach."

A thrill of nerves went through me as a thought reignited my fear. If the goblin could look like Dr. Gremhahn and look as different as the fisherman, couldn't he look like a man driving a new Buick? Wouldn't that be a good trick—to scare us with fog and birds and then pretend to be our savior?

I reached for Mother's arm, but she was already climbing into the sedan's back seat at the same moment John Hayden was sliding behind the wheel. She scooted across, making room for me to sit. I glanced at the driver, who was watching us over his shoulder with the merest hint of interest, and then at Mother. I climbed in.

I thought the man would strike up a conversation, but he stared ahead and drove without another word. I wanted Mother to check her compass, to make sure we weren't flying down the road with the sea goblin himself, but she seemed content to lean her head back and close her eyes. When, after a long silence, John Hayden suddenly said, "Where in Long Beach would you like to be let off?" I nearly jumped out of my skin. Mother opened her eyes, sat forward, and said, "The beach past the amusement park would be perfect. Thank you."

It was only then I realized Mother held the compass in her hand, had been holding it a long while, maybe all along, since I hadn't seen her reach into her bag to get it. So I guessed I'd worried for nothing all this time that we were riding with the sea goblin.

And realized that I no longer doubted the existence of the gremhahn or the rightness of our quest.

John Hayden maneuvered the car down a narrow road that ended at the ocean. Mother and I got out. She walked over to his window, which was down, and was about to say something when he put up his hand to stop her.

"Diana Hasbro and I are old friends. She asked me to keep an eye out for you and offer assistance if I could. I've been driving back and forth on this road for two days looking for y'all. I'll be glad to head home now."

"Oh," Mother said, evidently as surprised by this news as I was. But it comforted me, this idea that the finder woman was looking out for us, still offering her help. It made me feel sorry that I'd thought badly of her, hadn't believed in her. And it made me think that maybe—if all these things I hadn't believed in were actually true—the finder woman was right all along, and Jimmy could be saved.

"And it was my pleasure, Ma'am," he said, flashing a big smile that made me ashamed I'd thought him to be the goblin.

"One last thing," he said. "Listen to what the seals say. They're on your side."

He pulled the Buick away from us and was gone.

"Oh," Mother said again.

I'm sure there was more to her thoughts, but they must have overwhelmed her because she went silent. She only went to the sand, took off her shoes, and walked.

"Why do you think he said the seals are on our side?" I asked as we walked along. The day was cooler than it had been all week, and the sand felt good beneath my bare feet. The ride had refreshed me, and my bags didn't feel nearly as heavy.

"Maybe because the ocean is their home, and perhaps the sea goblin takes baby seals as well," she said.

"You're guessing."

"Well, yes. Of course I'm guessing." She smiled. "Maybe it wasn't true seals at all he was talking about. Maybe he meant we have selkies here in California. Folk who are seals in the sea but who can take off their skins and be human on land. The Irish and the Scots are full of tales about them."

"It would be a very long swim from Scotland to California," I said, playing along as I tried to visualize a seal as a human. "They would be funny-looking people, don't you think? Short arms and big round bodies."

"They say," Mother said, "that selkies are very handsome in their form. It's said a human woman can't resist a selkie man. Selkie women are supposed to be docile and make good wives."

45

"Humph," I said. "Sounds like men made up the stories to suit their liking."

Father certainly hadn't liked it when Mother had made her own decision to go to the finder woman. Though that was odd, come to think of it. He'd always encouraged her fancies before and was proud that she had gone to college—not many women did—and had a degree of her own. It was part of the change after his illness. It seemed he didn't like her having her own mind and thoughts anymore. He certainly didn't want her acting on them. Which made me worry again about what he would think if he came to the house and found it empty.

"Did you send Papa a message to tell him we'd be away?" I asked.

Mother didn't seem surprised by the change of subject. Perhaps her thoughts had strayed to Father as well.

"I wrote him a letter," she said. "I told him we were going to visit your Aunt Betina for a few weeks and I would contact him again when we returned."

Good, I thought. One less thing to worry about.

We'd walked a long way while we talked. The beach was narrow here, barely any beach at all between the boardwalk and the sea. Shrieks and screams rolled down from a nearby amusement park with a big wooden roller coaster that rose up behind the beachfront buildings. The aromas from food stands made my stomach rumble. We hadn't eaten since breakfast and now it was leaning toward evening.

"Maybe we could get something to eat soon?" I said. "And I hate to say it, but I need a toilet."

Mother consulted the compass again and sighed. "He's gone west, into the water." She scanned the beach, emptying now that the sun was setting and the wind coming up. "Where do you suppose we are?"

"Seal Beach," I said. "I saw a sign with the name on it."

"*Seal* Beach," she said, emphasizing the first word, as though it held some portent, given what we'd been talking about. "I don't see any seals here, certainly don't hear any like we heard at the cove, but I do see that big ol' roller coaster."

"The park is called Joy Zone," I said. "I saw a sign for that, too."

She smiled. "*Seal* Beach and Joy Zone. Those are good omens, don't you think? Let's find a place to eat and then a place to sleep. Should be plenty of both around here." She chucked me under the chin. "And a toilet."

⁓

*W*hen Mother checked the compass the next morning, the goblin was still at sea and so far away the compass face was black as pitch. The next day was the same, and the day after that. On the morning of our fourth day in Seal Beach, Mother and I walked down to the water. It was too early for Joy Zone to be open, but from behind the wall we heard the workers calling to one another and the sounds of test runs on the still-empty rides. I smelled fresh popcorn being made. In front of us, the ocean rolled small, gentle waves onto the sand and then sucked the water back out again.

"What if he's still far away?" I asked.

"We'll wait here," she said firmly. "This is his last known landfall. He'll return to this place."

But of course that was just Mother trying to impose her will on the sea goblin. He could make landfall on Catalina Island, or Alaska, or Japan for all we knew. Maybe he liked to spend the summer months in Tahiti.

She took out the compass but hesitated to open it. I guessed she doubted her own brave words.

"He's come back," I whispered, to give her hope, even though I doubted it myself. "Take a look."

She flipped open the cover and peered at the instrument. "You're right. He is back. But gone north now, near to where we started, to judge by the hue of the compass face."

"Oh," I said, and put my arm around her. "Oh."

This whole week had been for nothing.

A worm of worry slithered through me, a fear that this quixotic quest would go on forever, us running up and down the coast until one of us dropped.

"Sometimes, Cassie," Mother said into my shoulder as though she'd heard my thoughts, "I think this hunt is madness. That the truth is your brother is in a cold grave somewhere and we will all go to our own graves never knowing what happened to him. I think, at these times, that there's no such thing as a gremhahn. That the so-called finder woman has played me for a fool and gained much of my jewelry and all of my sanity in the game. I fight the feeling away. I have to believe, you see. I *have* to believe."

"He did cure Papa," I said, suddenly seeing the absolute truth of it. I straightened away from her, to look into her eyes. "It wasn't coincidence that Papa's fever broke and he was suddenly as healthy as he'd ever been the very morning after Dr. Gremhahn came. And there's his name. I went to the library, the big one in Los Angeles—rode the trolley there —and looked it up. There is a folk tale about the gremhahn, a seagoing troll or goblin that can change its shape to look pleasing to humans. It steals children."

I left off there. I wouldn't tell her the rest of it—that the gremhahn makes a meal of the stolen child. I didn't tell her that I had believed it was all coincidence.

That I'd believed that whoever played the doctor at our door and the finder-woman were in it together—along with

John Hayden and his fine big car—and I cursed myself because I was the one who said we should go see her.

Sometimes I thought we should tell the police that the "doctor" had kidnapped Jimmy and that the "finder woman" surely knew where he was being kept, and all the police needed to do was force her to tell the truth.

I couldn't fathom why Mother and Father hadn't done that. Why they let the police fade away in their inquiries without so much as a mention of the "doctor." I suppose it was the length of time. More than four years had passed between Father's cure and Jimmy's disappearance, and there was only my word that I'd seen the doctor on the beach that day. Maybe they thought the police would dismiss that as coincidence or the overactive imagination of a teenage girl.

Or maybe Mother hadn't wanted to admit how much of her jewelry had disappeared into the hands of a woman claiming to sell a magic compass and a binding spell.

"We'll find him," I said firmly, putting shut to any linger doubts I might have. "We'll bring Jimmy home."

FIVE

Seal Beach, California
August 1923

A glint of something silver half-buried in the sand caught my eye. I reached down and plucked up a small triangle of paper.

"What have you got there?" Mother said.

There was nothing written or drawn on the silver side. I turned the paper over and read the printing.

"It's part of a railway ticket," I said.

"To where?"

The paper was torn but I could read the destination. "Chicago."

Mother sighed. "I was hoping for a sign. I was hoping the ticket would tell us where to go next."

"You don't think the sea goblin would go to Chicago?"

Mother shook her head. "I suppose he could. He could take human form and ride a train, but why would he? So far all his torments for us have been ocean-based. I don't think we're meant to chase off across country."

I didn't think that, either. To be honest, it wasn't really a thought so much as a feeling—I *felt* that the gremhahn was tied to the sea. *Felt* it so strongly that even though I wasn't the type to go strictly on intuition, I knew we were meant to stay on the coast.

"So, today?" I said.

Mother glanced at the compass.

"Time for us to go," she said. "We'll fetch our bags and check out of the hotel."

"And head where?"

"Home," she said.

I stared at her, my eyes wide.

She shrugged. "The compass says the goblin is far from us now. It doesn't say where he is, of course, but I feel he's gone back where we began."

"You feel it?" I said, skeptical, even though I'd just felt something so strongly that I believed it completely.

She half-laughed. "I know. It's not like me to go on intuition alone. But—" She hesitated a moment. "I trust the magic."

There was a sentence that would have made me laugh out loud not too long ago. Now I simply nodded.

Mother smoothed my hair back from my face. "We'll take the train. No more walking for a while. So, back to the hotel for our things."

"And to change?" I said, eyeing her trousers. Dresses and gloves were more appropriate for the train.

"And to change," she said.

At the Pacific Electric Railway ticket counter, Mother smiled at the counter man and clicked open her coin purse. "Two tickets to Hermosa Beach, please."

"Are you really sure about going all the way back home?" I said quietly, doubt now dissolving my belief in Mother's intuition. "What if we go too far and miss him?"

She took the tickets and we walked toward the platform.

"Remember, I can tell how near or far we are from him by the color of the compass face. I'll check all the time we're on the train. If we go too far, we'll get off and go the other way. But the magic tells me to go home. I think, no, I *feel* that somehow the gremhahn is strongest in Hermosa. He's led us on this chase, but I *feel* he's realized his own mistake and is seeking to remedy it. "

"That's good," I said. "If he's made one mistake, he may make more."

The train pulled into the station and we got on board with our traveling bags. There were few people on board, and we found two seats in a section we had to ourselves. Mother and I both removed our hats and settled in for the ride.

As the train pulled out of the station, I stared out the window and sighed. I needed to believe that the goblin had shown himself to us that day on the beach. To believe he'd taken my brother. That the finder woman was looking out for us, and the seals were our friends. I needed to believe we'd get Jimmy back and would all be one family again.

When we came into Long Beach, Mother took out her compass and checked it. "Still farther on," she said.

As the train pulled out again, I asked the question that had been rolling around in my head for days, "Do you miss Papa?"

Her lower lip trembled a moment and she swallowed hard. "I miss the man I married. I miss the man who fathered you and James, giving me the greatest gifts of my life."

I heard the "but" coming.

"I don't," she said, "miss the creature who hit me and left us."

She took my hand gently in her own. "Do you miss him?"

I nodded. "I do. Not every day anymore, but often. I missed him long before he left us."

Mother nodded. She knew what I meant—that after Father recovered from the flu, he was never really the same, a difference that grew and grew until he was the angry, screaming man who'd hit Mother and left us at the beach when he went back home. My friend Moira, who lived on our block, had written, saying Father had a new lady friend. I told her I didn't want to hear anything more about it, and she'd not mentioned it again. When he came to visit and bring Mother her money, I pretended I didn't know.

"Did you ever think," I began, then stopped. "Did you ever think it wasn't the flu that changed Father, it was the doctor?"

Mother tightened her hold on my hand. "I'm sure of it. And it drives me even more to find the goblin and give him what he deserves."

A cold shiver ran through me at her words. I thought of the large carpet bag she'd carried on this journey, how Mother took it aside when she needed to open it, and never let me see what was inside.

I thought about it a long time, while small towns, wild land, and cultivated fields passed by, and realized that Mother not only wanted to find Jimmy, she hoped that somehow defeating the goblin would restore her husband as well. That it wasn't only my dream that we would be a whole family again—it was her dream too.

If we shared that desire, wasn't it possible that deep in his heart, new lady friend or not, Father did, too?

When we couldn't see the ocean, Mother would check her compass obsessively, sometimes shaking it—I presumed because she'd lost the reading. Finally, with a deep huff, she'd shove the thing back into her handbag.

"Mama," I said carefully, wondering if this was the right

time to broach my future. "I think I'd like to go to college next year."

Mother's face lit up, but before she could respond a couple came down the aisle and sat in the seats facing us. They were about Mother's and Father's age, I guessed, and well dressed, though there was something just a little off about them. I couldn't say what—maybe it was the big hemp sack bulging with shapes of who-knew-what inside that the woman lugged up onto the seat next to her, or the way they sat with us when there were other open seats all around, or the way the woman immediately caught my eye and smiled like she knew me.

"Going far?" the man asked, looking straight at Mother.

"San Pedro," Mother said, which was several stops away, but at least it was westerly. I wondered why she hadn't said our true destination.

"We've been in Tijuana," the woman said. "George likes the horse races."

Mother nodded politely. She didn't like gambling of any sort—except, weren't we taking a gamble now, trusting the finder woman and the magical compass?

"Won big, too," George said.

"Do you often go to Mexico?" I asked, also being polite. Both of my parents had drilled manners into my head.

George looked at his companion. "Marlys here loves it down there. She strolls on the *playa*—that's beach in Spanish —while I go to the races." He smiled at his wife and then shot a glance at the large sack next to her. "And she loves to shop."

Something was moving in the bag, wriggling inside it. I stared and then glanced up at the couple. Marlys smiled, opened the sack, and drew out a small brown dog with big bulging eyes.

"I call him Pepe," she said. "He was running around on the street. I caught him and put him in the sack, to contain him."

She smiled again, stroking the little dog in her lap. "Anything that needs catching and containing, a big burlap sack will usually do the trick."

The train slowed, coming into a station.

"Well, here's us," George said, and stood.

Marlys didn't put the dog back in the sack. Instead she pushed the bag to George, who picked it up, while Marlys continued to pet the dog in her arms. The two made their way down the aisle and out the door without another word to us. I peered through the window and spotted them on the platform. Marlys gave a tiny wave in my direction and then they were gone.

"Mama," I said as the train began to move again. "What if we put the gremhahn in a sack? Would that be a good way to control him and make him do what we want?"

I could see her thinking.

"Yes," she said. "I think a large sack would quite do the job." She patted my hand. "That's a very good idea, Cassie."

I grinned inside myself, happy to have contributed something more than companionship on this quest.

～

"Come on," Mother said when the train pulled into Wilmington.

On the platform, she faced west, took out her compass and frowned.

"We're not close at all, according to this."

Mother stood tall and looked around, trying to see over and through the crowd of people on the platform. "Where do you suppose the taxi stand is?"

"Where are we going?" I asked.

"Oh," she said. "I see it. Over there. You see?"

She started off and I trailed after her.

The driver took our bags and stowed them away, asking, "Where to, ladies?"

"What I need," Mother said to the driver, "is to buy a large burlap sack. Do you know where I can do that?"

The driver stroked his chin. "A big one? Like for a three-legged race?"

"Exactly." Mother seemed to seize on the idea. "We're on the planning committee for the church picnic. The sack race is always so much fun, but over the years the sacks—well, they do wear out eventually."

I kept my eyes straight ahead. We attended very serious-minded churches—one by the beach and one near the big house—both selected by Father because the congregational makeup was good for his business. I'd never been to a church picnic in my life.

"You're in luck," the driver said. "My wife is on the committee here at Saint Pat's. I know exactly where to get some."

"What good fortune we came to your cab," Mother said, and gave him her most gracious smile.

The driver pulled away from the curb. Mother leaned over and whispered in my ear, "I don't know what got into me. I never lie like that. Must be the fairies' influence." Then she winked.

~

Back on the train, Mother was serious again. The big burlap sack we'd bought was rolled tight and tucked into her carpetbag. She kept the compass out all the time now and checked it every few minutes, turning her body always to the west. I could feel the anxious energy pouring off her like waves of steam.

"Are we close?" I asked, my voice low even though no one

was sitting near us. I kept glancing around, half expecting to see George and Marlys suddenly appear again.

Mother drew her lips into a tight line, then heaved a loud sigh. "I believe we're going right back home. I'm sure that's where he is. Right back where he stole my baby."

I turned my gaze to the window and beyond. The sun was moving west. By the time we pulled into our station, it would be sinking toward the sea, the sky alight with pinks and oranges, blues and gold. If Mother's compass said the gremhahn was near, she'd likely hunt him in the dark. I hoped for a bright moon and no clouds.

We stepped off the Red Car at the station where Hermosa and Santa Fe Avenues met. We could walk the few blocks to our house from here. The fresh air and the act of walking would help clear my head, I hoped. I longed for a warm bath and my own bed. Chasing the gremhahn just to wind up back where we started had exhausted me.

But Mother was having none of it. She checked the compass again, stomped her foot the barest bit and said, "Right." The next thing I knew, she had marched into the Berth Hotel at Tenth Street and the Strand, dropped her bag by the check-in counter and slipped Jack Masters, who was manning the desk, a quarter to watch our things. Then she marched back out onto the Strand with the big burlap sack stuffed inside her carpetbag.

The light was beginning to fade. I swallowed hard. Chasing the gremhahn in the dark didn't seem like the best idea.

"Mother," I said, grabbing her arm. "I've had a terrible thought."

She gave me her full attention, probably as much because I'd called her Mother, which I hardly ever did, as the idea of my terrible thought.

I dropped my voice low so the end-of-the-day tourists

dragging their beach umbrellas, buckets, shovels, and tired children past us back to wherever they would sleep that night wouldn't hear my words. "The gremhahn can change shape, look like whoever or whatever he wants. How will we recognize him? He might look like the doctor or the fisher-man, but he might not. He could look like anyone—a young man on the beach, or a small child, or an old man or woman."

Or a flock of angry seagulls, I thought, but didn't say.

"The compass will tell us," she whispered back. "And I have a secret finder as well. One I haven't told you about. It only works when we're close."

Mother opened her carpetbag and pulled out a small white box. She carefully lifted the lid and showed me what was inside—a wide silver ring with an amethyst the size of the tip of my finger set in it. "I'll wear the ring. The stone will glow brighter the closer we come to our quarry."

I swallowed. *Our quarry.* I wondered again what Mother had in her carpetbag that she wouldn't let me see.

I'd worn a pair of black T-strap pumps with short heels on the train. As I bent to slip them off, I caught sight of some people I knew from school, likely down to the beach for the day, standing in front of the bowling alley. One of the girls, Cynthia, from my American history class, caught my eye and gave a small wave.

She must think I'm crazy, I thought, in my white lace traveling dress and no stockings, slipping off my shoes right by the sand, my mother doing the same.

Mother put the ring onto her finger, squared her shoul-ders and marched onto the beach. I glanced back at Cynthia and the others, gave a little shrug, and followed Mother.

SIX

Hermosa Beach, California
August 1923

There were fewer and fewer people on the beach as we drew closer to the water. Mother kept her eyes on the compass and made minute changes in her direction based on what she saw there. We walked toward a group of young people, my age or thereabouts, but no one I knew. I hoped the gremhahn wasn't hiding as one of them. I didn't like the idea of my mother attacking and stuffing someone my age into a burlap bag. Though, of course, the sea goblin wasn't my age at all. Did creatures of that sort even have age?

I was relieved when Mother glanced at her ring and walked right past them. I felt their eyes on us, their eyebrows raised in curiosity as we passed in our traveling dresses, shoes in hands, Mother's head bent over the compass. She headed toward a barefoot man in his early thirties, I guessed, with dishwater hair and sharp features. He wore loose trousers and a light-blue open-collar Danton shirt, and stood alone on the shore, staring out to the water.

A commotion behind us made me turn my head to see the group we'd just passed packing up and leaving. In moments, it would be only the man and us for as far as I could see up and down the beach. I looked over my shoulder at the Strand. People there could see us now if they paid attention, but we'd disappear from view once we reached the tide line beyond the dunes.

Mother looked up from her compass, consulted the ring, and put her finger to her lips to warn me to be stealthy. She quietly opened her carpetbag and withdrew the big burlap sack, spreading open the top. She reached in again and handed me a long length of rope, which I'd not seen before.

The waves were growing raucous as the tide came in. I didn't think the man heard us at all as we snuck up behind him. But he heard Mother's yell as she leapt for him. He started to turn, likely to run, but she was fast, so fast I couldn't believe it. She threw the bag over him and her arms around him.

"Quick," she said to me, and I stretched the rope around the bag—which wasn't easy since the goblin was struggling inside and cursing like a sailor.

Mother had her arms around him and I had to thread the rope between her and the sack, but I managed it, pulled the knot as tight as I could, and then knotted the rope again.

"More at the feet," she said, still holding on to the squirming gremhahn in the bag.

Mother intoned the binding spell while I wrapped the rope around his feet. I tied that off with a double knot as well. Only then did she let go, and the sack, with the sea goblin in it, fell over onto the sand.

Mother fell on him, her eyes wide and crazy in the hazy evening light.

"Give me back my son," she screamed, while hitting the gremhahn all around his head and shoulders with her fist.

Hitting him hard. Harder than I would have thought her capable.

She broke off for a moment and glanced at me. "Get the steel bar in my carpetbag."

My heart pounded. So that's what she had in her bag, what she'd planned all along to use on the gremhahn.

My hands shook as I pulled it from her bag, not sure I wanted to be part of beating someone. No, not someone, some thing. A thing that had changed my father for the worse and stolen my brother.

The bar was about eighteen inches long and had spikes on one end. I couldn't imagine where she'd gotten it.

She took the spiked bar from me, her lips curled back over her teeth in a way I'd never seen a human do. There was something wolfish about it. And something of a lioness defending her cubs.

She raised her arm high and brought the bar down hard on the gremhahn. The harsh thwack of the blow made me wince.

"I," she said calmly, bringing the steel bar down.

"Want." Mother hit him again.

"My." Another blow.

"Son," she screamed, and hit him so hard I didn't know if the goblin could survive it. A red stain spread along the side of the burlap bag.

"Stop. Stop," he cried, "and I will do what you ask."

A gremhahn, I had read, was a sneaky creature, prone to lies, but Mother had pronounced the binding spell. He had to speak the truth.

"Let him out," I said softly, putting my hand gently on her shoulder. "It'll be all right. He can't lie to us. Let him out."

Mother stood back, breathing hard, her hands on her hips, the steel bar held tightly in her right hand. She nodded her head, and I undid the rope around his feet and then the rope around his chest and arms. He sloughed the sack off like a disgusting skin. Blood seeped down his arms from the blows Mother had dealt him.

"Give me back my son," Mother said again, her voice as hard and unbending as the steel pipe.

"Your boy is right here," he said, much too lightly for my comfort, and reached into one of the large, loose pockets of his trousers. He pulled out a seashell that was white and bumpy on the outside, with long white spines protruding here and there, the inside as smooth as oil and apple-blossom pink.

Murex ramosus. I knew it because we'd had a course on the sea and seashells my junior year in High School. I knew, too, that it didn't belong around here. It was a South Seas shell, not one for the California coast.

Mother looked at the shell a moment, her mouth hanging open, her breath coming fast and hard. Then she hit him again on the side of the head with her fist.

"What lie is this?" she demanded, even though a bound sea goblin had to tell the truth.

Did the binding spell not work? Had she gotten the words wrong?

"No lie," he said, rubbing the spot where she'd hit him with his free hand. "Call him if you don't believe me."

Mother gritted her teeth and let no words pass them.

"Jimmy," I said. "Are you there?"

A small voice came out of the shell. "Here, Cassie. I'm in a little pink room and I can't get out."

Mother sucked in a deep, shocked breath, then hit the gremhahn with her fist again, saying, "Return him to where he belongs. Return him right this second or I will beat you with the steel bar until you are nothing but little pieces and I will feed those pieces to the seagulls."

The goblin bowed low, and then straightened. "As you

command," he said, and cocked back his arm and threw the shell into the ocean with all his might.

I watched the shell arc through the air, flying over the sand and past the foaming waves to drop into deep water.

"What have you done?" Mother screamed, and grabbed the gremhahn, shaking him so that his head bobbled back and forth.

"What you bade me do, Madam," he managed to say. "Returned the shell to where it belongs."

Mother drew her hand back to hit him again, but the sea goblin twisted away and scrambled free.

And began to grow.

Taller and wider he grew, until he was much too big for Mother to hit or control in any way. He looked down on us from his great height.

I could see his anger before he even spoke—the clenched fists, the bulging eyes. When he did speak, his voice was like rusty pieces of metal scraping one against the other.

"You, Madam," he said, "will never see your son again."

He looked down at me. "But you might, little one. And, oh! I have some special things for you."

"No," Mother cried out. "You've taken my son. Don't curse my daughter as well."

"The boy is mine," the gremhahn said. "I will do what I will with him. The girl is yours, but I am not cruel. I will give her a gift: one tiny star shall light in her hair for every month she lives from this day forward. A tiny star to remind her of the day she was cruel herself, and her mother more cruel to this poor gremhahn who wanted only what was his by rights."

He turned and bolted toward the sea, his form growing smaller and changing with each step until he was more fish than man, running on his tail fin. He reached the water's edge and turned back to us, calling out, "I nearly forgot. Girl, you shall never know marriage or motherhood. Why? Because if you should ever know a man, the moment he enters you, you will dry up and become dust."

The sea goblin was all fish now, a grayish-brown color, the scales dry but somehow glittering even though it had become night and the light on the beach was dim and watery. An ugly, ugly fish standing on its fins as if they were feet, its wet, glassy eyes staring at Mother and me, the two of us staring back, my heart pounding in my chest.

He leapt into the sea and was gone.

SEVEN

Hermosa Beach, California
September 1923

I started my senior year not at my regular school in Los Angeles but at the high school in Redondo Beach, the next town over, since Hermosa didn't have one of its own. My old school had shut down during the Spanish flu while the school at the beach hadn't. As a consequence, I was older than everyone else.

Some people said I was older because I was stupid and was held back. My grades put shut to that story in a hurry. There was a funny rumor that I was even older than I looked, that I was the film star Bessie Love, doing research for a new movie. People often said I resembled her. It was the hair, I thought—long and wavy.

Except these days I mostly wore it pinned in a bun or tucked under a hat, to hide the two stars that gleamed there. Every morning as I carefully pinned up my hair, my stomach knotted and anger burned in my heart for what the gremhahn had taken from us, my brother, Jimmy, and what he'd left us with in return—Mother to never see her son again; me to never know love, marriage, and children of my own.

And yet I couldn't dwell in that angry land, much as I wanted to. To seethe with fury gave the goblin more power over me, and I would not give him that. I pinned up my hair and got on with my life as best I could.

Thanks to Mr. Moses Sherman—who'd developed the Red Car trolleys that ran absolutely everywhere—five days a week, my arms laden with books and a sack lunch I made for myself, I was able to ride to school and back rather than walk. I didn't know very many of my fellow students, and that was good, because I sped straight home every day alone. I didn't want anyone inviting me to their house. It simply wasn't possible. I couldn't leave Mother home alone all afternoon and into the evening.

How could I explain to a friend wanting to visit that ever since the gremhahn had cast my brother into the sea, my mother hardly spoke and mostly stared out at the ocean. That even as she cooked dinner, her eyes would stray away, her mind far from where she stood. That my father had left us. That he only occasionally stopped by to bring us some money and ask how we were doing, then left again. That I worried about them both. That they'd each grown gaunt and seemed much older than they had at the beginning of summer.

I went to school and studied hard and worried about Mother. Life had narrowed down to that.

~

*N*ovember slunk in cool but calm, but had turned blustery within days. Mother didn't seem to notice the drizzle or the wind. She stood on the porch in front of our house, staring out to sea, no different this day than any other in the months since the goblin had thrown Jimmy's shell into the ocean.

Except that autumn had come, and rain with it. Mother didn't pay it any more attention to the weather than she did much of anything these days. Throughout the waning days of summer, beachgoers had occasionally given her looks as they passed by, Mother standing as still as a mountain or sitting practically immobile in one of the two wicker chairs I'd put on the porch for her. I fetched her coat from the closet and took it to her.

"Thank you, Cassie," she said as she slipped it on.

"What do you expect to see out here?" I asked, finally broaching the question that had rattled in my head for a while, though I wasn't sure I wanted the answer.

She turned her head slowly to look at me. "Your brother, of course. He's a clever boy. He'll escape the kidnappers and come home to us any day now. I want to be here, waiting for him when he arrives."

I blinked in surprise. Looking for the gremhahn, looking for another chance to make him give Jimmy back—that's what I'd thought had been consuming her these past months, eating her up inside, devouring her mind.

Molly had died while we'd been on our quest, and that had devastated Mother as well. Neither of us had ever properly grieved her death, and I think that ate at Mother, too. I knew it ate at me, a second hole burning next to the one reserved for Jimmy. There was a hole where Father had been as well, but at least he was still alive and well.

"You know Jimmy is in the shell, and the shell is in the ocean," I said softly.

She pressed her lips together and gave her head a small, fast shake. "What are you talking about? What shell?"

"Nothing."

The rain started falling in earnest. "Why don't you come inside now? We'll leave the front door unlocked. Jimmy can come right in when he gets back."

She shook her head again, meaning *No* this time.

"It's not right, Cassie. Jimmy will have worked hard to escape and return. He shouldn't come home to find us drinking hot chocolate in the kitchen as though everything were fine. He needs to know we've been waiting."

"I'll bring an umbrella, then," I said, and went back to get it. Out front again, I opened it and handed it to her. She took it and held it over her head.

"Go inside," she said. "No point both of us standing out here."

Later, when I looked out the window, Mother had let the umbrella fall to her side and stood in the rain, her sopping dress clinging to her skin, staring at the sea.

$\sim$

"*P*apa," I said tentatively, holding the handset of the phone in my hand as though it were made of spun sugar and might disintegrate at any moment, "I'm worried about Mother. She has a terrible cough and feels weak, but she won't let the doctor come."

There was a long bit of silence on the line before Father spoke.

"Why?" he said. I hadn't heard his voice in a while and his calm, never-ruffled physician tone felt soothing in my ear.

"She says she doesn't trust doctors anymore. That they are evil in disguise." A thought struck me. "Not all doctors. Not you. Just the local ones here at the beach."

Another silence, this one longer. "No. Why did you call me about this?"

It was my turn to go silent, to realize what I heard in his voice wasn't really calm—it was detachment.

"You're a doctor and her husband," I said, matching his demeanor. "She'll see you. She'll listen to you. I'm very worried. You must come."

Father's long sigh was audible over the crackling line. "All right. Tomorrow evening."

"Not sooner?"

"Tomorrow evening," he said again. "I can't come tonight."

"All right. Thank you." I hung up, only partially relieved. I put on the kettle for tea, hoping the hot liquid and steam might relieve some of Mother's congestion.

~

Father didn't appear until a little after eight the following night. He looked the same, but not the same—tighter-wound, as if he hadn't laughed in years. I wanted to put my arms around him, but this Father was not the same one who'd bounced me on his knee when I was a child, not the one who'd driven me to school every morning for years, private time for just the two of us to talk or sometimes sing silly songs. This was not a father I could hug or ask about his obvious unhappiness. This was Dr. Goodlight attending a not-favorite patient.

Mother had again insisted on sitting on the porch all day, but she'd let me bundle her in blankets and would drink the hot tea I brought her every hour. She was in bed under a white goose-down comforter when Father arrived. He strode toward her room, his bag in hand, that "professional" look on his face where I had hoped for kindness and care.

"Good God, Audrey," he said when he opened the bedroom door and saw her lying there, this once-robust woman now tiny and bird-like, barely making a bump under the comforter, and heard the wet, rasping wheeze that passed for her breathing these days. He rushed over, felt her forehead and took her pulse.

"You should be in the hospital," he told her. "I'm taking you, right now." He turned to me. "Get her coat and put a small bag together for her. She likely will be there a while."

I did as he said while he got her sitting up and listened to her heart and lungs with his stethoscope. That was just motions—him doing what a doctor did, when he'd already determined how very sick she was and likely had named the ailment in his mind, if not out loud.

Mother didn't fight or complain as we helped her to Father's car—he had a new one, I noticed, a pea-green Lincoln sedan—and got her settled in the passenger seat. I opened the back door to get in, but Father said, "There's no reason for you to go, Cassie. You can't help and I would rather have only one woman to worry about at a time."

His words stung. I opened the passenger door again, kissed Mother's burning cheek and said, "I'll come tomorrow to visit you."

He waited impatiently for me to finish my good bye, and then a thought seemed to hit him.

"Where's the dog? Where's Molly?"

I swallowed hard. "She died a while back. I thought Mother wrote to tell you."

"No," he said. "She didn't."

If you'd called, I thought, *asked to speak to me, I would have told you. But you didn't. Not once. Mother and I found the gremhahn but lost Jimmy a second time. When we went to fetch Molly home, Mrs. Lou said she'd died while we were gone. She felt terrible about it. I cried for days for Jimmy, for Molly. My heart was ripped up and thrown to the winds, Father, and you never called.*

He switched on the ignition. "Well, then—"

"Is Mother going to be all right?" I asked, dropping my voice low.

Father's voice boomed out. "With proper care, she'll be fine."

He drove away without another word.

~

 $\mathcal{M}$ other got lots of proper care in the hospital—nurses bustling in and out of her private room, a luxury afforded her because of who Father was, bringing liquids to help with the cough and to let her sleep, and pills for the infection—but she wasn't fine a week later, or a week after that.

I rode the trolley downtown to the hospital every day. It was a long ride, rumbling along the tracks, with cars and pedestrians jostling for space on the street. Often I was the only passenger boarding at the Hermosa Beach stop, with more passengers coming on as the Red Car traveled north along the coast to Santa Monica. At Santa Monica I changed trolleys to go east into downtown, this car filling up more the closer into the heart of town we came. I didn't like the quiet of the seashore ride. It gave me too much time to think and worry. A crowded trolley was better, the noise and the crush of people a welcome distraction.

When I arrived on the fifteenth day, Father was in Mother's room when I came to her door. I saw him through the little glass window. He sat in the same ladder-back chair I always drew up next to her bed during my visits. His bag was at his feet and he held her hand.

I slowly, quietly pushed the door open, took a step inside and stopped. Father didn't seem to notice me. There was no tensing of his muscles to betray an awareness of my presence. I took a few more steps. He didn't turn. The room was private but small. A few steps more brought me next to him. He turned his head then and gestured with his eyes to a second chair and then to the spot next to him. Without a word, I picked up the other chair, set it beside his and sat down. Father still held Mother's hand. His gaze had returned to her face. He reached out to take my hand in his free one. Tears sprung to my eyes and I blinked them back. I'd missed him so much.

"How is she?" I asked, my voice barely above a whisper.

"The same," he said, his voice as quiet as mine had been.

The same. Which likely meant that he'd been visiting her all along. He wouldn't tend her; he'd leave that to another doctor, one he trusted. Father always said that a physician should never doctor anyone he cared about—that emotion got in the way of best medicine.

"Why the same?" I asked, my voice inching toward normal. "She's been here weeks and getting good treatment. Why isn't she getting better?"

Father's voice creaked when he answered. "I don't know, Cassie. Sometimes with pleurisy . . ." He turned my hand loose and ran his hand over his tired face. "Maybe we caught it too late."

My breath caught in my throat. He cared about her. He loved her still. That woman he had at the big house was nothing to him, not in the way Mother was his heart. All that needed to happen now was for Mother to get well and we could go back to being a family again.

Almost a family. A family with a piece missing—a hole that could not be filled.

But a family still—if only Mother would get better.

"It's not your fault," I said. "Not medicine's fault, either."

"What do you mean?"

Unconsciously I reached up under my hat and touched one of the stars in my hair. It lay on a strand that fell right

74

behind my ear. There were four now, as hard and cold as diamonds, their glow faint but enough that I kept them hidden. It wasn't Father's fault, nor medicine's—all blame lay at the gremhahn's feet.

I shook my head at Father to say I couldn't explain what I'd meant. He would never believe what I'd come to accept— the sea goblin was draining Mother's life force. The gremhahn had said she would never see her son again. If she died in the hospital, his curse would be true.

Father said, "I've convinced Dr. Johnson to send to Boston for a new drug. They've had some good results with it. It's being flown here especially for your mother. We'll have it in a few days."

"You broke your own rule," I said, half teasing, needing to see him smile. "You interfered in the care of a family member."

His eyes narrowed and his jaw hardened. "Perhaps you would have preferred I left your mother in your capable care —where she most certainly would have died."

His words hit me like blows. I leaned back in the chair. It was almost as though the sea goblin stared out through my father's eyes, spoke through his mouth. Was Father's kind-ness an act, or was the sudden cruelty forced on him by the gremhahn?

Father blew a harsh breath out of his nose, then reached out and gently touched a strand of hair that had escaped from under my hat.

I stiffened, afraid he would feel a star, but they were secreted under my hat, away from prying eyes and kind hands alike.

"You're right," he said. "I did break my own rule."

"Good," I said, and hoped it would be good. Hoped that Mother would recover. That medicine and love were stronger than dark magic.

~

*O*utside in the hallway, Father slumped against the wall, worn out and exhausted. He'd never let Mother or me see him this way before. He had always come home at the end of the day and gone straight to his study for thirty minutes. No one was to disturb him during this time. Decompressing, he called it. Exactly thirty minutes later—I could have set my watch by it, and Mother did in her way, timing dinner so that it was set on the table exactly one minute before—he would emerge and we would eat together. She'd said people didn't need to say "I love you" all the time if they showed it every day.

But he was tired now. He ran a weary hand over his face again, as if he could rub fatigue away with his palm and fingertips.

"You love her," I said quietly.

He nodded. "Always have. Always will." He glanced my way. "Always loved you, too."

"Then why?"

He sighed. "I don't know, Cassie. At the time, when your mother told me she was determined to look for Jimmy, I suppose I went a little insane. It was the futility that made me crazy, the heartbreak I knew would come to her."

He paused then, and sucked air over his teeth thoughtfully. "No. It started before then. Since right after I had influenza, I suppose. Anger buzzed in me like bees swarming around the hive. I couldn't name a reason for it, but it was there every day and night. Over time it grew and grew until that day—" He looked away from me. "The day I hit your mother and abandoned you both."

He paused again. "After, later, when the anger went away as quickly and with as little reason to go as it had had to come, I was embarrassed. My behavior was unacceptable, but

I was too proud to apologize and ask for forgiveness. And now, here we are."

I put my hand gently on his arm. "I've missed you."

"I've been thinking," he said. "With your mother ill, you shouldn't be alone at the beach house. You don't even have Molly anymore. You're completely by yourself there. You should come stay with me."

My heart leapt and then fell. "Isn't . . . she there?" More words followed in a rush. "Don't be angry. Moira told me about your girlfriend. That she lived at the house. Lives there."

He nodded. "Belinda, yes. She's there, but you're my daughter. You come first."

Would he kick her out for me? Did I want that?

"I'm fine at the beach house," I said. "And I am nineteen. I can live where I please."

"True," he said. "I hoped it would please you to come stay with your father."

I saw then how lonely he was, even with Belinda. Saw that in some way he thought my being at the house would bring Mother back to him, too. That he wanted what I'd wanted—for us to be a family again.

"I'll bring my things tomorrow," I said.

~

*M*y stomach was tight as I walked past the sentry line of Spanish firs that hid the house from the street. The taxi driver lugging my trunk whistled through his teeth when the house and the large yard studded with tall queen palms came into view. The house itself was no grander or more impressive than others nearby, though it might have seemed that way after the rather dramatic entranceway. Father had designed the house himself as a scaled-down version of a mansion he'd seen in Spain while on a respite from the war.

To me, the house looked as it always did—the two-story, white stucco walls with red roof tiles in the Mediterranean style. Red damask drapes hung in the tall windows on the first floor. Large swaths of the front wall stood hidden by purple-red bougainvillea and the white oleanders I'd been warned never to touch.

I saw the refined beauty of the house and understood why both Father and Mother loved it. For me, home—the place my heart felt most at rest—was the beach cottage, and always would be.

I paid the cabbie at the door, thanked him, and tipped him extra for helping with the trunk. I opened the front door and called out a tentative "Hello." The woman who came from the direction of the kitchen wasn't Sophie, who'd been our housekeeper for as long as I could remember, but a stranger. My shoulders tensed, wondering if this tall, stern-looking blonde was Belinda, my father's live-in girlfriend.

The woman's face remained about as expressive as an ice cube as she approached me.

"You must be Cassie," she said in a strong Swedish accent. "I am Inga."

Not Belinda, then. My shoulders relaxed.

"Mr. Goodlight said you'd be arriving," Inga said. "I've prepared your room." She glanced at my trunk. "Someone will come later to bring that up."

Seeing a place you know well but haven't seen in a while can be odd. My room looked the same and yet foreign. The canopy bed and white eyelet lace bedspread I'd loved as a young girl seemed childish now. Why was my plush zoo and wooden horse collection still on display? It had been five months since I'd last stepped into this room, but it seemed decades. Only the books crowding the shelves they stood on still felt like familiar friends.

The thump-thump of my trunk being dragged upstairs startled me. A blond about my own age appeared, though I could only see him from the back as he lugged the trunk into my room. He stood and turned around.

"This is my son, Franz," Inga said, and frowned at me.

Franz was handsome, no denying that, and I thought Inga's frown was a warning to stay away from him. Unconsciously, I reached up and touched the spots where, under my hat, stars glittered in my hair. A tight knot formed in my stomach. Inga didn't have to worry about me.

Where was Belinda? Waiting downstairs to ambush me? To tell me how sorry she was about my mother but that she was sure all would be fine in the end? Or to complain how my father was spending much too much time at the hospital? The spacious room felt suddenly hot and close.

"I'll put my things away later," I said, edging toward the door.

Inga nodded, and she and Franz moved aside so I could flee. I hurried down the stairs and out the front door, turned left and walked fast toward Moira's house.

Moira welcomed me into her house with a quick hug.

"Are you moved back in?" she asked when we'd settled ourselves in the parlor.

I hadn't been here in a while, either, but the sameness of the brown leather sofa that had adorned this room for ages, the two club chairs upholstered in blue brocade, and the old, marble French clock on the mantel that had been there for as long as I'd known Moira were comforting.

I shook my head. "My trunk is there, but I can't do it. I want to, for my father's sake, but—

Moira tilted her head, a few of her springy red curls falling over her forehead, waiting for me to go on.

"Everything *looks* the same," I said, "but nothing *is* the same."

"Is your father home now?" Moira asked, smoothing her curls away from her face.

"Still at work."

"So you could make a quick getaway, if you wanted."

The thought was tempting. "I can't do that to him. I said I'd come stay. I want to run, but I can't."

"His house is closer to the hospital," Moira said, as if trying to find the silver lining. "How's your mother?"

"The same," I said. "Father has ordered some special medicine for her. It's being flown here from Boston."

Moira jumped to her feet. "I have an idea. Have Inga tell your father you forgot a few things and are going back to the beach house overnight to get them. That'll buy you another day at least. I'll drive you."

I thought it over. Father would understand one more day.

"There's something creepy about Inga," I said. "Have you met her?"

Moira laughed. "Oh yes. And the handsome Franz, who she claims is her son but the neighborhood is sure is her lover."

"Moira!" I said, not as shocked as I should have been, I supposed.

"The raven-tressed Belinda brought in Inga after Sophie quit in a huff. Sophie declared to all and sundry that she would not work in a home where such immoral goings on were occurring, and she would never take instructions from a hussy." Moira said.

She grinned at me. "I see you smiling. I'd be pleased by the story too, in your place."

To be honest, it did please me that Sophie had refused to work with Belinda in the house. It might have been only a moral question for Sophie, but I suspected that loyalty to my

Mother had more than a little something to do with it as well.

But I saw now that telling Moira I didn't want to hear any more about Belinda had meant I'd cut myself off from knowing what was going on in my own family. I wouldn't make that mistake again.

It'd be good to be with Father again, but not quite yet. Belinda, Inga, Mother still deathly ill in the hospital—I wasn't ready to take all of it on at once yet.

"Another night in Hermosa would be welcome," I said. "More time to get used to the new arrangements."

"Excellent," Moira said, sweeping a warm shawl over her shoulders. "Give me a moment to tell my mother, and then we're off."

~

I dreamed of Molly that night, tucked up in my bed at the beach house. A short dream, Molly crawling into bed with me the way she used to, her warm furry self stretched out beside me, my arm around her body, her chin on my chest. She gazed at me with her deep brown eyes and whimpered. In the dream I asked her what was wrong, tried to comfort her, but it was no use. She whimpered and cried, cried and whimpered, and then the dream was gone.

~

*T*he morning broke sunny and beautiful, the cold rain evidently banished until real winter would set in. Even before I got out of bed I heard beachgoers passing the house, their chatter and laughter as they headed toward their day's outing.

Moira had left before breakfast, needing to get to her job.

While I ate, I wondered how much more to pack. I couldn't know how long I would be with Father—until Mother was well? After Mother was well? Mother and I both with Father for the rest of our lives? I should have thought of these questions yesterday.

I was still thinking when the phone rang and I got up to answer it. A woman was sobbing on the other end.

Oh no, I prayed, not Mother. But no one calling from the hospital would sob, no matter how bad the news.

"Ma'am," I said. "Ma'am, are you all right? You've reached the Goodlight residence. Can I help you?"

"Is this Cassie?" she managed between sobs.

"Yes," I said. "How can I help you?"

There was more sobbing. Clearly this woman had meant to call me, but I had no idea who she was or why she was carrying on so.

"Ma'am," I said again. "Ma'am?"

"He's dead!" The woman screamed at me. "He's dead and I don't know what to do. Your father is dead."

For a long moment I couldn't think, couldn't speak, could only listen to her sobs.

I realized this must be Belinda. I tried out the name.

"Belinda, what happened?"

"Hit by a car," Belinda said, not screaming now, but her words tumbling out as if they might trip over each other. "Run down. I was right there beside him. He was dead before the ambulance came."

My mind froze. It wasn't possible that he was dead. Not Father. He was big and strong and would live forever. But he was dead. Molly had tried to tell me it was coming.

I shook the thought away. I had to think.

"What am I going to do?" Belinda wailed.

That was the question, wasn't it? So many, many things to do suddenly.

"Belinda," I said, using her name again to make her focus, "where is he now?"

I could hear her swallowing, trying to get control of herself.

"They took him to McCormick's funeral home."

I nodded, but of course she couldn't see that over the telephone.

"My mother, his wife," I emphasized the word to make our positions clear, "is in the hospital."

"Yes, I know," she said. "I'm very sorry she's ill."

She sounded sincere, which made what I'd say next a little harder.

"I know you live at the house. I don't want to leave you immediately homeless. Take two days. Pull your things together. Find a place to live. Do you have a key to the house?"

"Yes," she said, shock clear in her voice.

"I will meet you there Thursday morning to get the key. Do not take anything of my father's. If you do, I will know. Mother and I will take care of everything. Do you understand?"

"Y-y-yes," she stammered.

"Thank you for the call," I said. "I know this is hard for you."

"Yes," she said again. There was a long silence, and then the sound of the receiver being put back on the hook.

I held the phone in my hand a moment longer, then set my own handset on the cradle. I sank into a chair and stared into space. Tears filled my eyes and a sob rose in my throat. I let them both break free.

≈

*M*other had always said I was too young for black when I'd spied some black blouse or dress I felt drawn to in a store. Nothing in my wardrobe was appropriate for a funeral—all pastels and jewel tones. A girl's wardrobe, not a woman's.

I sighed and went into Mother's room. We were nearly the same size, though I was a little taller. I chose a black, drop-waist dress with cap sleeves and only a moderate amount of bead decoration. I found a pair of black gloves in Mother's dresser. I might look more like I was headed to a party than a funeral, but at least the color would be right.

I held the dress a moment, thinking this was probably the first big decision I'd made without benefit of counsel from one or both of my parents.

No, that wasn't true. I'd made the decision to give Belinda two days to get out of my father's house. I'd fired Inga and Franz. I'd dealt with the funeral home, made all the arrangements, and gone to the bank and convinced the manager to give me access to my parents' accounts. I'd notified the hospital, my father's nurse and office manager, his personal friends and important business acquaintances. I'd gone to the hospital and told my mother that her husband was dead. I guessed I was old enough to wear black now.

~

*T*he turnout for Father's funeral was more than I expected. Nearly two hundred people came. Some I knew—doctors, nurses, orderlies, business acquaintances, Father's best friend since grammar school, our longtime housekeeper, Sophie—and many more whom I didn't. Belinda had the good sense to stay away, though I thought I'd spotted her, a bouquet of white lilies in her arms, lurking at the back of the church and then later at the cemetery.

Pastor Timmons, whom I'd known nearly all my life, led the service. John Gilbert, Father's oldest friend, gave a eulogy full of funny stories from their youth. Two gentlemen Father had served with in the Great War spoke of his compassion and his bravery under fire. In a way, it was death that finally, fully restored to me the father I'd known and loved.

As I walked out of the National Cemetery onto Sepulveda Boulevard, the last person to leave the graveside, a man stopped beside me on the street.

"I'm sorry about your parents," he said.

"Father," I said. "Were you a friend or business acquaintance of his?"

"Parents," the man said again.

In that shocked moment as I realized what he meant, I saw a cab coming and hailed it. Inside the taxi, I looked out the back window just in time to see, where the man had stood, a seagull rising into the sky.

"First and Hill Streets. The Receiving Hospital," I said to the driver. "Hurry please."

We raced down Wilshire Boulevard, past the Ambassador Hotel and Cocoanut Grove, past MacArthur Park, the cabbie swerving around automobiles and trolley cars. We turned on Figueroa, and then onto Second Street, and finally, finally onto Hill. All the while my mind spun with only one word: *Mother.*

EIGHT

Los Angeles, California
November 1923

I burst into Mother's hospital room, my heart pounding and my hands shaking. The smell of bleach used for cleaning was faint but distinct in the air. My eyes swept around the small room, taking in the white walls, the small dresser, silver radiator, and the slim bed with iron head and foot rails in which my mother was resting. She looked at me from the bed and smiled.

Not dead. In fact, sitting up and looking better than she had in weeks. For a moment I couldn't grasp it and felt more stunned than relieved. Why had the man made me think Mother, too, had died or was dying? What was the point?

Panic, I supposed. The man, whoever or whatever he was, wanted me frightened and worried. To feel the horrible pain of believing I'd lost both parents.

I was sure it had been the sea goblin who'd made her ill. Why would he frighten me with intimations of her death but

87

let her regain her health? Did he have some other, worse plan in mind for making sure his curse came true and Mother never saw her son again?

"Cassie," Mother said, her voice strong and cheerful. She held out her hand. "Come help me to my feet. The doctors say I can go home today. I'm completely cured, practically overnight. The doctors say they've never seen anything like it."

My heart shuddered in my chest. How could she be so quickly and miraculously cured except by the gremhahn's sorcery—the same way Father had been cured, years back? This miracle was no gift, I was sure of that. Had we paid in advance with Father's life?

Maybe the sea goblin wasn't responsible for her illness or her recovery. If the gremhahn hadn't made her sick, maybe he also hadn't addled her mind so that she stood in the rain and got sick. Maybe that was worse. It was better that the sea goblin had made Mother unhinged than that she'd become unhinged on her own.

"Was it the medicine that Father sent to Boston for that did it?" I asked, taking the hand she held out to me.

Mother nodded. "Dr. Johnson said it was. He's sent to Boston now for more. Evidently I wasn't the only person to come down with a very bad pneumonia this year." She held out her hand.

I helped her to her feet, thinking I was glad it was the medication and not the sea goblin that had saved her. Though that didn't mean it wasn't the gremhahn who'd sent her out into the rain to get sick in the first place.

Mother leaned against me, still weak from her illness and the long period in bed. I braced myself to support her and wrapped my arms around her, happy that she was alive and gaining back her health, whatever the cause.

She rested her head on my shoulder. "I wish I'd been this

much better yesterday," she said quietly. "I should have been at your father's funeral today."

"He never stopped loving you," I said. "He was here every day."

"I know," she said. "Even when I was deeply sleeping, I knew he was here, felt his hand holding mine, his kiss on my cheek."

She stiffened then, holding back her sobs. Her face was against my shoulder, and I couldn't see the pain there. I felt it, though, thrumming though me the way the clang of the biggest, deepest-voiced church bell echoed inside you long after the ringing had stopped.

Mother drew in a deep breath, straightened, and took a step back to look me in the eyes. Hers were dry and clear. And firm—the eyes of a person who'd mapped out her future.

"We should move back home," she said.

"The big house?" I shook my head, not wanting to think of the implications but needing to ask. "What about Jimmy? You made yourself sick standing in the cold and the rain so that when he came home, he would know we'd never stopped waiting. Now you want him to return and find the beach house empty?"

Mother sank back onto the bed, sitting on the edge, her hands folded one over the other in her lap. "It's time for me to move forward, Cassie."

"Why this change?" I said.

She held her breath a moment before answering. "I learned things while I was ill. I can't tell you yet. I need time to think it through, to understand."

I stared at her.

She smiled weakly. "Let's go home. Both of us. To the big house."

I rubbed the side of my face with my hand, thinking.

Mother continued before I could answer, "Both you and James were conceived and born in that house. I loved your father and you and Jimmy there for years longer than our time in Hermosa Beach. I've never felt at home at the beach the way I do on Cicada Lane."

"I didn't know that," I said, drawing the words out slowly while my mind spun.

"As for that woman, Belinda—" Mother snapped her fingers, a loud cracking sound. "She's as gone as some house-cleaner that came in once or twice when you were young. She means nothing."

There was no point in protesting. Mother was going back to the big house, and that was that. First Father and now she seemed to be drawing me back there as well, but it wasn't where I wanted to be. Still, I could stand it for a while. It seemed to mean much to her.

I cleared my throat. "Let's focus on getting you out of this hospital. I'm sure you're ready to be shut of it."

"I am that," Mother said. "My bag is already packed and the bill paid. Let's go home."

~

Mother threw herself into being Dr. Goodlight's widow the way she'd thrown herself into the hunt for the gremhahn. She joined the Friends of the Library and plotted a charity event for children orphaned by the Great War who were now old enough for college. She tore out the rose bushes in back that we both guessed Belinda had planted, since Mother hadn't and neither of us saw Father as a rosarian. She replaced the rose bed with a vegetable garden filled with rhubarb crowns and, since it was winter, started strawberries in the greenhouse. Evidently pie would be on the dessert menu in the future.

I knew Mother could throw herself wholeheartedly into whatever cause or quest she chose, but I couldn't help feeling that she, like Father, had come back from her illness changed. Even if it was for the better, she was someone else now. And likely enough, so was I.

~

Two weeks before Christmas, Mother and I piled into the pea-green Lincoln sedan for the short drive to Father's lawyers and the reading of the will. I hadn't known she knew how to drive—Father had always taken the wheel—but she drove now with evident relish and a bit more wild abandon than I would have hoped for. I thought I understood her recklessness—the pending division of Father's possessions made his death more solid and final somehow.

Mr. Grayson, the head of the firm, sat with Mother, me, and three other lawyers around a long walnut table. I'd known that as a family we were comfortably well off, but not so well off as the reading of the will revealed.

Father had collected properties and buildings the way some men collected stamps. And, true to Father's precise nature, he'd been very specific as to what percentage of the banked savings were to go to Mother, to me, and to be held in trust for Jimmy, along with which properties each of us received. Mother was named executor of Jimmy's portion until he was either found or declared dead, at which point Jimmy's share would be divided equally between her and me.

Mother inherited the big house, as expected, but I was surprised that he'd left the beach house to me, free and clear. I supposed he'd known how much I loved it, and he didn't want it sold away from me. A small bequest, which I didn't begrudge, went to Belinda with his thanks for the comfort and companionship she'd provided him.

On the drive backe I said, "Did you know Father was leaving the Hermosa house to me?"

Mother nodded as we skidded around a corner, and I held tight to the hand rest to keep from tumbling into her.

"I knew how the will was set up," she said once we were going straight again. "Except for the money to Belinda, of course."

She pulled to a stop at a Red Car crossing and said, "You should take what's yours and move back to Hermosa."

Her words so surprised me, I couldn't reply.

"I know what you've been thinking," she said, taking off again once the trolley had passed.

"You do?"

Mother nodded. "You think that since my illness I've changed. And of course you're right. I lost my husband suddenly to an accident while I myself lay near death. Things like that change a person. Puts things into perspective. I was wrong to drag you around searching for the sea goblin and Jimmy. I had no right to pull you into it."

"I wanted to find them as badly as you did," I said. "It's my fault the gremhahn even knew Jimmy existed. He saw us on the beach and came that night to steal him away. If I hadn't been so anxious—"

"That's ridiculous," Mother said. "It's no more your fault than it was mine or your father's. The fault lies with the thief, not with those stolen from."

She was right, but it didn't lessen the guilt I felt.

What I said was, "I'm glad you took me with you. I'm glad I was there to see you beat the sea goblin with a steel bar. I know that's wrong, that vengeance belongs to the law and to God, but really, Mother," I laughed slightly, "you were magnificent. It felt lovely to hear him cry for mercy."

"For all the good it did," Mother said, turning onto our block. "We lost Jimmy a second time that day."

"In our minds, at least," I said, broaching a subject I knew was tender. "But what if Jimmy was lost when the goblin first took him? What if the thing with the shell was a cheat, a game the goblin was playing?" The words were tumbling out, coming faster and faster. "And the curse he laid on me, that could be nothing. Probably is nothing. I know the goblin is real. I know we saw him change into that big ugly fish and dive into the water, but the rest of it could just be cruelty on the gremhahn's part. Jimmy's—"

"Dead," Mother said as she pulled into our driveway. "But he's not." She turned the car off and laid her hand on top of mine. "I have changed since the illness. I see things now with a clarity and certainty I've never known before. I know Jimmy is in the sea. I know I should live here, in the home I shared with my husband and children. I know you should live by the ocean, have your own life. You might think it would be the other way, you should live here, with all your old friends around, and I should live at the beach and hunt for my son. But that's not what fate has in mind. We each have our part to play, and we cannot take the other's role."

"Mama," I said, and stopped. She was rambling and her words didn't make sense. Maybe I should call her doctor. Ask him to come to the house, see if she was all right, really all right. I couldn't think about her being sick that way, in the brain.

"Cassie," she said, "I'm not losing my mind. When I was ill I fell, one day, into a sudden, no-reason-for-it unconsciousness. While I was unconscious I had a dream. Not a dream, actually, but a vision. Everything that will happen was laid out in front of me."

My breath caught in my chest. It was one thing to use

tools like the compass and the ring to find the gremhahn—quite another to start seeing the future in fever dreams.

"Do you remember," she said, "what I told you just before we left the hospital? That I'd learned things but couldn't tell you until I'd had some time to think about it? The vision is part of what I was talking about. I needed time to determine if it was a function of being sick or a true thing. I know now it was true."

"Okay," I said. "Can you tell me the vision?"

Mother hiked one shoulder in a bit of a shrug. "I was under a tree on a green, grass-covered hill. The day was warm but not hot. A man walked up and said, 'Don't worry about not finding your son. He's waiting for you, but his sister will find him, not you.'"

"And then?"

"Nothing. That was it. But I *knew* more than what the words said. I knew I should move here but not keep you with me forever, as much as I want to. If you'll be the one to restore Jimmy to us, you need to be in the sea goblin's territory, and that's the ocean."

"Who was the man?"

Mother shrugged again. "A fairy? A guardian angel? His wasn't a face or voice I knew from this life."

If I hadn't seen the gremhahn turn into that giant fish with my own eyes, I might think my mother was completely insane. As it was, what she said sounded like truth. Her words settled over me like a robe that grew heavier the longer I sat and thought about them.

"It's not your responsibility," Mother said. "It's something that will happen in the course of your normal life. If you searched for the gremhahn now, it would be wasted effort. You need to live your life and give it no more thought. Finding Jimmy and bringing him back to us will come naturally, if you let it."

That was a relief at least.

"Am I right that you'd rather be at the beach house?" Mother said.

I nodded. "I'm sorry."

She waved my concern away with a flick of her hand. "Cassie, you're nineteen, a grown woman. I was engaged to your father at your age. It would be selfish of me to keep you from stretching out into your adult life. You can visit, of course."

"I will," I promised. "All the time. I'd miss you too much if I couldn't see you, talk to you like always."

Mother opened the car door on her side. "Good. It's decided then." She paused. "Aren't you and Moira going to the movies tonight?"

Guilt twinged in me but I nodded. Moira and I had plans, but not for the movies. She'd convinced me to come with her to a jazz club called Mimi's, where she said the music was hot and the young men sublime. That the club served illegal alcohol and could be raided at any time didn't seem to worry her.

~

"You're not going to wear that, are you?" Moira said when I walked into her room. She eyed the blue dotted Swiss middy blouse and white skirt with knife pleats I'd changed into at Mother's.

"I'm supposed to be going to the movies, remember?"

"Good thing we're about the same size," Moira said and threw open her wardrobe doors. "Pick something."

Moira's father was a banker and her mother high society, and Moira dressed the part. My own wardrobe wasn't lacking, but Moira's put mine to shame.

"You pick," I said.

Moira grinned. She loved clothes and had firm opinions about what worked best on all our friends. She rifled through the nicer dresses, segregated from the everyday frocks, and pulled out a sleeveless rose-pink chiffon dress with a handkerchief hem and handed it to me. She looked down at the plain black pumps I was wearing.

"Nothing we can do about the shoes," she said. "But you wear that dress and no one will be looking at your feet."

Moira and I had shared clothes all through high school but never shoes, since I wore a size larger than she did.

She was already wearing the embroidered gold shift dress she'd chosen for the night, and as soon as I had changed, she hustled me out the door for our night on the town. Her parents had gone out earlier for some society do, and neither the maid nor the cook had popped her head out of the kitchen when I'd come in. Neither did now as we left.

The club was in a nondescript gray building in downtown Los Angeles. The windows were covered as if the building were abandoned. Moira knocked, whispered something to the man who opened the door and slipped him some money. He stood aside, allowing us to enter a dark hallway that gave me the shivers. Moira obviously knew her way, and I followed her to another door that opened into the club itself.

The light dazzled me. The sheer number of people squeezed into the large room made me feel a little queasy. On a small stage at the back of the room, a mixed band of Negro and white musicians were playing "Home Again Blues," and many of the people, mostly white but some Negro and a few Oriental couples, were dancing. Those not dancing sat at small round tables covered in white tablecloths, set around the perimeter of the room.

This is a mistake, I thought, liking the music but not the

rest. Too loud. Too bright. Too much color and laughter and women with cigarettes in long holders, men in tight-fitting sacque suits, everyone trying to impress everyone else. Father would have hated this place, too.

I sighed. Maybe if Father hadn't died so recently I'd see Mimi's with different eyes, curve my mouth into smiles, let laughter flow from between my lips.

Moira grabbed my hand. "Come on," she said, pulling me toward the bar at one side of the room. "Geeze, you look like I dragged you to school on exam day and for once you're not prepared."

"Sorry," I mumbled as we came to the long dark-wood bar. Mirrors ran the entire length of the back, visually doubling the number of people dancing, drinking, posturing.

"A gin rickey, please," Moira told the bartender, a hard-faced man in his forties who glared at her a long moment before turning his harsh gaze to me.

"Champagne," I said.

The man turned to get our drinks.

"Champagne?" Moira said. "Since when do you drink champagne, my teetotaling friend?"

I shrugged. "Since tonight."

Moira huffed out a breath. "Good for you. I hope you feel like dancing. A few of the gents are already looking our way."

I glanced around the room again. There were a number of young men who seemed not to have dates, and I thought dancing might be nice after all. It had been a while since I'd had fun and, dammit, I was here for a good time and I would have it. I might even laugh if a young man said something witty and amusing. I couldn't remember the last time I'd really laughed, and I very much wanted to.

The band swung into "Hot Lips" and I found myself tapping my foot to the music as I looked around.

My perusal of the room stopped when I spied a man standing by himself near the stage. He was the most beautiful human I'd ever seen—brown hair, brown eyes I thought, but it was hard to tell at this distance, tallish, and he filled out his suit quite well. There was something rugged about him that put me in mind of the sea, but of course he could easily have been a ballet dancer or office clerk for all I knew. Maybe he felt my eyes on him, because he suddenly looked up, straight at me. I looked away and busied myself watching the bartender fill my glass with champagne. When I glanced over again, the man was no longer by the bandstand. I surreptitiously looked for him, but he seemed to have vanished.

The band was launching into a Dixieland piece and I'd barely sipped my drink when a tuxedoed man with a pencil moustache jumped onto the stage and motioned the band silent with his hand.

"Ladies and gentleman," he called in a loud voice. "I do apologize, but we've just been notified that some uninvited guests of the law enforcement type are on their way. If you would kindly exit." He swept his arm to indicate another man, who pulled a curtain aside to reveal a door. The door wasn't far from the bar. Moira swallowed down the last of her gin rickey, grabbed my hand, and with the rest of the crowd we sidled out of the building.

We found ourselves in an alley. People were scattering in both directions away from the club, like bats from a cave. I have a pretty good sense of direction and after a moment's orientation knew which way to go to retrieve Moira's car. I nudged her and began moving the way we needed to go.

"Can I offer you a ride?" a man's voice behind us said. A voice as smooth as melted butter and honey.

I turned and saw the beautiful human. Up close he was even more breathtaking. Older than me, but not by much. I'd been right that his eyes were brown, a color so rich and deep they seemed almost unnatural. My throat was suddenly very dry and I swallowed hard to relieve it.

"Paxton Yeager," he said, with a small dip of his head as he introduced himself.

Moira seemed struck dumb. She stared at Paxton Yeager, her mouth a little open, but no words came out.

"Thank you, but our car is nearby," I said.

He dipped his head again, turned and walked in the opposite direction.

Moira grabbed hold of my upper arm.

"Why did you say we had our car?" she said. "He would have driven us home, or maybe to another club. We could have come back and gotten my car tomorrow. My parents wouldn't even have noticed." She glanced back at the place where he'd stood. "Did you see him? That is the most dreamy man I've ever laid eyes on."

I frowned. "I didn't know that your parents wouldn't notice. My mother would have a fit if I took the car out and didn't return with it. Besides, he could be anyone—a murderer of silly women who get in his car, for all we know."

Moira rolled her eyes. "Honestly, Cassie. Have you no adventure in your soul?"

We drove home with Moira singing "My Man" a few times through, as if she were Fanny Brice, followed by "I Ain't Got Nobody" and "There'll be Some Changes Made." I sat quietly through the songfest, thinking of the beautiful human and how, if the law had come, Mother would have been more upset because I'd lied to her than that I'd been arrested. I thought, too, about her vision that I would be the one to find Jimmy. Now, how was I to do that?

~

*T*he next morning Mother drove me to Hermosa. Moira came along to keep me company for a few days while I adjusted to having the house to myself. I'd thought I'd already adjusted while Mother was in the hospital, but when she came into the cottage and started packing up her belongings, a new aloneness filled me. I was glad Moira, at least, would be there for a while.

～

I walked with Moira to the Red Car trolley stop, both sad and happy she was going home. Sad because she was fine company, happy because the days had given me time to think and to adjust to my new life by the shore. I waved as the Red Car pulled away.

The day was lovely, the deep blue sky dotted with wisps of white clouds scudding east, blown by the ocean's winds. The sun was as bright as a lemon, the air neither cool nor hot, but a perfect warm—too nice a day to go back inside right away. I strolled the beach south, walking at the water line, picking up an interesting mussel or wedge clamshell or sand dollar now and then.

The tide was coming in. Water lapped around my ankles and calves as waves tumbled onto the shore. Winter waves were the rowdy older brother to summer's gentle waters. An unexpectedly large wave nearly knocked me off my feet. When the water receded, my heart seemed to stop and then pounded like a jackhammer. Lying at my feet was a large, white shell—*Murex ramosus*.

More waves washed around my legs as I stared at the shell, half afraid to touch it. I glanced west and saw another large swell on its way in. A wave that could maybe wash the shell back out to sea. I bent and snatched it up, then ran above the tide line to dry sand.

It was nearly Christmas and, despite the nice weather and school being on break, few people were on the beach. Still, I hunched over to hide what I was doing and brought the shell near my mouth.

"Jimmy," I said softly into the pink heart. "Are you there? It's me, Cassie."

NINE

Hermosa Beach, California
December 1923

I put the shell to my ear, but heard nothing other than the normal reverberation of surrounding sounds, which people claimed was the echo of the sea.

"Jimmy? If you're there, say something, anything, or just make a noise. Anything to let me know I've found you." All I heard was the false-repeat of ocean waves.

Was this a trick by the sea goblin? Throw an empty shell at my feet and make me hope my brother was inside? My teeth clamped together and my jaw tensed. This gremhahn was a cruel beast.

A seagull flew overhead, screeching its raucous cry, then diving to snatch a bit of crust from a sandwich left on the shore. I reached into my pocket and threw the largest clamshell I'd found at the bird, and was pleased to see it fly off squawking, without its crust.

I took the *Murex ramosus* and went home.

~

*T*hat night I slept little. I lay awake, fingering the stars in my hair—there were five now, hard, cold reminders of the gremhahn's cruelty. I wanted to rip them out of my hair and grind them into dust.

Why deposit that shell at my feet? What did the sea goblin want—only to cruelly tease and frustrate me? Was there another, more sinister reason behind it?

In the morning I ate, dressed, and called for a taxi. Mother had said finding Jimmy would come in the natural course of my everyday life, but the sea goblin didn't seem to agree. Whatever his ultimate intent, he wanted my attention. The shell had done the job admirably.

I didn't use Mother's trick of going all the way to the top of the hill and walking back down. I went straight to the finder woman's house, walked up the drive and boldly knocked on her door.

Diana was clearly surprised to see me. Before she could speak, I burst out with the reason I had come.

"Please," I said. "Will you teach me magic?"

Diana smiled sadly. "Oh, Cassie. No one can *teach* you magic."

I stared at her, my mouth hanging a little open. This wasn't the reply I'd expected, though honestly I didn't really have expectations—only hopes.

"Then sell me something better than the compass and the ring," I said. "Something that will make the sea goblin come to me, and a way to make him give back my brother." I paused a moment, thinking of the diamond and emerald brooch in my handbag, left to me by my grandmother on Father's side. "I can pay."

Diana sighed. "Cassie, come in and we'll talk."

I followed her in. Besides the brooch, I'd brought a ruby

ring and a necklace with a waterfall of moonstones. I'd gladly part with them all to get my brother back.

"You don't seem to realize how this all works," Diana said as we walked toward the front parlor. "Yes, I could sell or give you an amulet to help you do what you want, but they wouldn't work for you."

"The compass worked for my mother. And the ring."

"Because once your mother discovered who she was, she also discovered how to make use of the objects I provided. Your mother is a *finder* as well. The compass and the ring are simply ways to focus and amplify her natural magic. Without inborn magic, the things are worthless."

Frustration bubbled in me. "That's exactly what I'm asking for—to learn the magic that will let me defeat the gremhahn."

Diana nodded toward the plush yellow sofa with lion-claw feet, and I sat down, my back as straight as a soldier, my hands clutched together in my lap.

She took a seat in a wooden chair opposite me. "I understand what you want, but you don't understand what magic truly is."

"It's a way of making things happen, of controlling events."

Diana sighed. "Spells and potions can make things happen, but spells and potions aren't magic."

I bit my lip. If Diana wouldn't teach me, how would I ever free my brother and restore my family? What was left of it, now that Father was gone.

Her face softened. "Cassie, dear, you don't even understand what magic isn't, much less what it truly is, but I can tell you that magic definitely isn't something you can demand or even ask to learn."

My heart fell. "So you won't teach me?"

"I can't teach you anything, but perhaps I can show you what is true."

She got up, turned, and walked toward her kitchen, motioning with her head for me to follow. The whole house seemed to take on an air of expectation. My heart hammered a little as I followed her down the hallway, with its parquetry floor and turquoise walls, into a large, tidy kitchen painted Dutch yellow. A large oak table and six chairs were parked against the left wall. A large butler's pantry opened off to the right. Herbs growing in pots filled the windowsills. I'd glimpsed the stove, sink, and icebox as I'd come in, but they were behind me now as I followed Diana deeper into the room.

The finder woman nodded toward the table for me to sit. She turned and went into the butler's pantry, reached up, and took a beaten-copper bowl down from a high shelf. The foot-wide bowl was shallow, almost a plate but for the gentle curve out and up. She also brought a bottle of murky water, set the bowl on the oak table, and poured the water into the bowl. It smelled briny.

"Ocean water?" I asked, and she nodded.

"Come," she said, "look at the water and tell me what you see."

I bent over the bowl. The water was cloudy with silt, though the heavier specks of sand were settling toward the bottom.

"Am I supposed to see something besides sandy sea water?" I looked up at her. My nerves were shooting warning signals all through my body.

"You tell me," Diana said, holding my gaze in her own.

I tore my gaze away and looked down into the bowl again, expecting to see the sea goblin in his lair, or Jimmy.

Nothing.

I glanced at Diana and turned my hands palms up. She motioned for me to try again.

The sand had settled to the bottom, giving the bowl the look of one of those beaches where the water is so clear you can see all the way down to the ocean floor.

And, like the water off those shores, there must have been some sort of tide in the bowl, because ever so slowly the sands were rearranging themselves into a pattern or picture. I watched, fascinated. I forgot Diana was standing near me and that I was in her house. A light breeze blew past my cheek. Maybe the breeze was blowing the sand bits? But that wasn't possible, since the water above them was still as a glacier.

Then not still. Slowly, almost too slowly to notice, the water started moving, swirling in lazy figure eights. As I watched, the swirls sped up. Small wavelets formed, with foam that peaked like whipped egg whites.

The water sloshed in the bowl, rising higher and higher on the sides until I worried the water and foam would rise over the rim and spill onto the floor. The egg-white foam stopped dancing atop the waves and began pulling together in a line across the center, seemingly not affected by the water still sloshing from side to side. The foam flattened and spread out, making a wing shape, with streaks of foam forming the feathers.

A seagull flew out of the bowl, almost hitting my face. I drew in a hard breath, threw up my hands and backed away. The bird flew around the room, screaming its raucous call. Diana was gone. She must have left me alone. But her abandonment wasn't nearly as frightening as the gull screaming and flying in circles around the room.

Then a new movement in the bowl caught my attention. Something else was emerging in the foaming water—a brown-furred seal, first poking its head, and then the top half of its body above the waves. A full-sized seal—impossible that it could come from the bowl, but it was. A seal with human arms, not flippers. And in its human hands, a bow and notched arrow.

The seal took quick aim at the seagull and fired. The arrow pierced the bird's breast, blood spreading across its breast feathers. The bird and arrow burst into a shower of sparks that fell over Diana and me, without burning us but sizzling as they fell into the water.

I turned and stared at Diana, who'd either returned or had never left the room, my body stiff and my eyes wide.

"What did you see?" she asked. There was no surprise in her voice at any of what had just happened.

I blinked quickly a few times, trying desperately to make sense of what I'd seen. But maybe there was no sense to be made of it. I'd come to the finder woman to learn magic—and magic was what had happened here. Nothing real. Only magic.

My pounding heart settled and I told her what I'd visioned.

She nodded, taking it in. "What do you make of it? Who or what is the seagull to you?"

I knew the answer but could hardly make myself say it. My words came out in a scared whisper. "The sea goblin."

Diana nodded again. "And the seal with human arms?"

"I don't know. Nothing, really." Then a memory came back. "When Mother and I were searching for the gremhahn, we saw seals off the beach, barking at the sea goblin who stood on the shore disguised as a fisherman. Later, a man who gave us a ride told us the seals were our friends. Mother told me the story of the selkies—seals in the sea, humans on land. I think it got all mixed together in my head and came out in the illusion."

"That could be," Diana said. "Now, the arrow—what do you make of that?"

I thought about it. Nothing else in the vision had been only what it seemed, so it was likely the arrow represented something, the way the seagull meant the gremhahn. An arrow is a weapon but also a tool. It could bring down an enemy or provide sustenance. I ran through the alphabets in my head, thinking maybe the arrow was a symbol for a word that sounded similar—arrow, barrow, carrow. I got to zarrow and hadn't found anything likely.

I guessed Diana could tell I was coming up empty. "Look within," she said.

I tried. Arrow could be Cupid's arrow. Love would kill the gremhahn? Was that why the sea goblin had cursed me to never marry? Some future husband would bring the gremhahn down if I wed?

I told Diana my thoughts, but she smiled and shook her head.

"You are the arrow, Cassie. You and you alone, though it seems you do have helpers."

"I will destroy the sea goblin?" I asked, remembering that Mother had said finding Jimmy was up to me. The two things could go together.

"Yes," she said. "It will come to pass."

"Will I get Jimmy back?"

"I don't know. There was nothing about your brother in the vision."

I licked my lips. "Can we do it again? I need to know about Jimmy."

"It wouldn't do any good. Your fate is your fate. It won't change unless you change the circumstance of your life. Even if you tried to change things, chances are you would still meet your same fate. Details may shift here and there, but you are the arrow and nothing can change that."

I sank down onto a bentwood chair with a round green cushion, and looked again at the copper bowl. The water was still now, the sand and silt settled once again on the bottom.

"Then I ask you again, please teach me magic."

Diana took another chair at the table. "No one can *teach* magic. You are either born magical or you're not. Magic either is or isn't in you. If it isn't, nothing will put it there. If it is—and clearly it is in you or you wouldn't have seen the vision—you can only look within for your particular branch of magic and do what you can to strengthen it."

"Is that what you did, what Mother did—strengthen a natural ability to find things?"

"Yes, that's my gift and hers. Your gift is different. You are vengeance and salvation."

I swallowed hard and rose to my feet, overwhelmed by all that I'd seen and heard. I needed time alone to think it through.

Diana saw me to the door. I walked home in a mental fog, knowing my way by habit. Vengeance and salvation. I had no idea what to make of that.

~

I thought about what the finder woman had said through most of a second sleepless night. It was Christmas Day. I put on a long-sleeved, grass-green day dress and low-heeled shoes, grabbed a green cloche hat, warm brown lambskin gloves and a black umbrella, just in case. I picked up the box that held the present I'd knitted for Mother, a new scarf and hat, and caught the Red Car.

The day was cool with the promise of rain in the dark clouds. Along with the Hermosa house, Father had left a sizable bequest to me. I could likely go many, many years not worrying about bills, and I thought I might use some of the cash to buy an automobile, so I wouldn't have to make the long slow ride to Mother's on the trolley.

Today, though, I was glad for the slow speed of the Red Car and, as we approached Los Angeles, for the thickening traffic that slowed the ride further. My mind whirled in so many directions, I wasn't sure I could have concentrated enough to drive. The best gift Mother could give me for Christmas was her levelheaded words to help me make sense of what had happened at the finder woman's house and all that Diana had said.

I got off at the closest stop and walked the rest of the way to the house where I'd grown up.

Mother was continuing to make the house hers, I saw. The stand of queen palm trees Father had planted and which had taken over the front of the house, blocking much of the sunlight from the yard, was gone. Where the palms had stood, behind the sentry line of Spanish firs, the yard was mostly brown dirt with a few strangled blades of grass. I could imagine how it might look in half a year, the lawn shining in the sun, as green as an emerald.

I stood at the front door a moment, wondering if I should knock. The beach house was mine and this house was hers, but did either of them belong to us both anymore? Did I expect Mother to knock if she came to Hermosa to see me, or to just walk in as always?

Don't be silly, I told myself and turned the knob, half surprised it wasn't locked, and opened the door. The house smelled of turkey and warm butter, sugar, and ginger—Mother had been baking. I called out just as I used to when I'd come home from school: "Prepare the victory feast. Your valiant daughter has returned!"

The pocket doors to the parlor drew back. Mother said, "And Merry Christmas to you, too." She threw her arms around me and we hugged for a long, lovely time.

As was tradition, I made the cranberry relish while the turkey Mother had cooked rested enough to be carved. We did our best to be joyous, but I'm sure Father and Jimmy were on her mind every bit as much as they were on mine.

Over mince pie I said, "I wanted to talk to you about something."

Mother raised her eyebrows but waited for me to go on.

"I went to see Diana, the finder woman, yesterday," I said.

Mother nodded. "Yes, I know."

"How do you know?" Had my mother added mind-reading abilities to her list of accomplishments?

"Diana told me about your visit with her," she said, "and what you saw in the copper bowl."

As if on cue, a knock came at the door. Mother gave me a sly smile. "I imagine that's her now." She glanced at a tray of cookies set out on the sideboard. "Bring the cookies and tea tray to the parlor, if you would, please."

When had Mother and Diana become such close friends that they not only spoke on the telephone but the finder woman had been invited to our house—on Christmas? Were they drawn together because they both had *finder* magic, the way strangers can become friends when they discover they went to the same school, even though years apart, or that they play the same instrument, or root for the same sports team?

Carrying the tea tray with the pot, three cups, and the cookies on it, I followed Mother into the parlor. She had made more changes here, too. Small ones. Moving a chair from the corner more to the center. Changing the cloth on the end table from the heavy brocade father had favored to a light, floral print. But mostly it looked and felt the same, like coming home.

Diana sat primly on the green velvet-covered horsehair couch, wearing a pleated brown skirt, white blouse, and brown argyle-patterned sweater, since the day was cool but Mother hadn't turned on the radiator. Mother was wearing trousers—not the ones she'd bought for our quest—and it made me smile. Father hadn't been gone long and I missed him, but it cheered me to see Mother coming into her own. From what little I'd seen, it didn't seem that Belinda woman had had any effect on the house at all.

I said hello to Diana, offered her tea, and settled into my usual chair, a rocker with a brown leather cushion—the same chair Mother had sat in to soothe us when Jimmy and I were babies.

"Diana called last night to tell me about your experience yesterday and your seeming determination to use your magic to bring Jimmy home," Mother said. "I felt this was something we should all discuss together."

I nodded. "Except she said she couldn't teach me—that no one could learn magic, it was either in you or it wasn't."

Diana set the teacup she was holding on the occasional table next to her. "That's true, Cassie. But—"

I sat forward. Sometimes *but* is the best word in the world —it holds out promise.

"But spells can learned by the talented. Spells that can help."

I knew this in the back of my mind. Mother had a spell to bind the sea goblin. When Diana had said she couldn't teach me magic, it hadn't occurred to me that she *could* teach me spells.

Mother nibbled on a ginger cookie, then held it in her hand. "Diana called to ask my permission to teach you certain things—enchantments."

Diana cleared her throat. "Of course you're of age and don't need your mother's permission, but what sort of friend would I be to Audrey if I didn't at least see how she felt about it before offering the knowledge to you?"

I looked Diana straight in the eyes. "Teach me." And then added, "Please."

I turned to look at Mother. "You don't mind, do you?"

"Mind isn't the word I'd use," she said. "I'd prefer you not chase the sea goblin, but it's your fate and nothing I can do will change that. I want you to be as well-armed as possible. I want you to do it right, not halfway, like I did."

My gaze shot from Mother to Diana and back.

"Your mother—" Diana said, and my gaze flew her way again.

"I got ahead of myself," Mother said. "I flew off half-cocked chasing the gremhahn. It made me a little crazy."

"Crazy?"

Mother blushed—something I'd never seen her do before.

"And then, all that standing in the rain," she said. "I was compelled, you know. I couldn't bear to be in the house. I know now it was undirected magic roiling around inside me that caused it." She shivered slightly. "It took a long time to get the magic settled."

So her illness wasn't caused by the sea goblin, but by an incomplete knowledge of how to use her magic. I didn't know if I was truly all that relieved to know this—not when I was begging to learn to channel magic myself.

"And then," Mother said, "it made me sick."

"Nearly killed you," Diana said harshly.

Mother nodded. "It did. So, of course I'd prefer that you not chase down that road, but I also know that I can't stop you."

I saw now what Diana was trying to tell me yesterday—that magic wasn't some trifling game. It was serious business and could have serious consequences. And yet—

I bit my lower lip and looked at Mother. "But you're all right now? The magic isn't still making you crazy or sick?"

"I'm fine, but I won't use magic again. It's not good for me."

I was relieved she was healthy, and relieved she wouldn't be using magic in the future, even though that was exactly what I planned for myself. I would have pursued learning the spells no matter what Mother had said, but it would be easier knowing that, even if she'd prefer things go differently, she had approved.

I faced Diana. "When will we start?"

"Tomorrow," Diana said. "Come to the house at noon."

TEN

Hermosa Beach, California
December 1923

I arrived at Diana's early, but not so early as to be rude. She'd invited me into the formal dining room and we sat at a walnut table that would easily seat ten, which seemed odd since Diana lived alone. I nibbled politely at the cucumber and watercress sandwich she had made and sipped the lemonade she served, trying hard not to scream my impatience to get started.

"This sort of magic, a magic that is akin to what the Hindus and Buddhists call karma, the bringing to someone what they have earned and deserve," Diana said, finally getting to the reason I'd come, "this magic has an odd component to learning how to make use of it."

I looked up, a crustless sandwich quarter poised in my hand.

"Until you reach a certain level, I can only teach you what you ask to learn," she said.

I set the food on its plate, the sandwich neatly obscuring

the red roses at the plate's center. "I'm not sure what you mean."

She gently pushed her plate away from herself. "If you want to learn something, you will have to ask specifically for a spell that does a specific thing. I can't guide you. It must be your own actions that drive forward your knowledge."

"I'll need to figure out myself what I need to know?"

"Yes."

"But eventually I'll figure out enough that you can start telling me what I need to learn next?"

"Exactly."

I don't know what I'd expected—that there was a book of spells and we'd start at the beginning and work through to the end, I supposed. I'd thought Diana would be the teacher and I the student, much like any class in school. I certainly hadn't thought this would be a self-guided course—that I would have to set the lesson plan when I had no idea what I needed to learn.

"How inconvenient," I said.

Diana's eyebrows rose at my comment, but she kept whatever she was thinking out of her voice. "What do you think you would need to learn first?"

I blew out a breath. "How could I know?"

She kept her voice pitched low, a calming tone. "Think of the steps. If you were to meet the goblin on the way home, what would you want to do first?"

"Grab him by the throat and make him return my brother," I said.

Diana's smile was kind, but I knew I'd given the wrong answer.

"Even before that, Cassie," she said. "Think."

Suddenly it was obvious. "I'd need a way to protect myself from him."

"And what might the way be?" she asked.

I thought about it. "Two things. One, a way to make myself invisible to the gremhahn. And two, a protective shield or something so whatever magic he threw at me would bounce off."

"Two good thoughts," she said. "Suppose we start with spells for those."

Another idea struck me. "And a way to hide the sea goblin and myself from being seen by anyone who might be around. A wide invisibility spell of some sort, I guess."

"Yes," Diana said, and then propped her chin on her fist, evidently thinking.

"Yes," she said again. "Come with me."

She led me out behind the house to a large swath of lawn beside a koi pond, stopped, and turned to face me.

"Put out your hand," she said.

When I did, she rubbed her palm over mine as if scraping something off her and onto me.

"Excorm," she said, and then, "You say it."

"Excorm." The word was neither Latin nor Greek, which would have made it easier to remember once I learned its purpose. *Excorm* was a nonsense word to my ears.

Diana nodded. "Good. Excorm is the spell word that will sheathe you in a personal protective covering."

I repeated the word over and over in my head, but said, "Don't I get a magic wand or something?"

Diana scoffed. "You're trying to be humorous. No magic wand, I'm afraid, but a hand movement—this." She turned her hand sideways and shook it once rather violently. "Try the word and gesture together."

"Excorm," I said, and twitched my hand the way she had.

"Very good." She seemed to be musing on what to teach me next. If every spell was as easy as that one, I'd be ready for the sea goblin in no time.

Diana strolled around the koi pond while she thought. She bent and picked up something she'd spied in the grass.

"Ow!" I cried, as a rock the size of a baby's fist struck my left shoulder.

"You must always be vigilant, Cassie," Diana said. "The protection spell must always be on the tip of your tongue."

I rubbed my sore shoulder and glared at her. "That wasn't fair."

Diana lightly shrugged. "The sea goblin won't be fair, either."

"Excorm," I said harshly, and flicked my hand.

Diana threw another rock. It hit me in the chest.

"This spell doesn't work," I said, rubbing the new sore spot.

"It works," she said. "But not when spat out in anger. You must be ready, but also in control of yourself, of the magic within you. Anger can get you seriously hurt. Or worse."

Or worse. Now there was a comforting thought.

I drew in a deep breath, held it. I let the air out, exhaling until my lungs were empty, then filling them again. It was an old trick for calming myself down.

"Excorm," I said, flicked my hand, and waited.

And waited, while Diana glared at me this time.

"I don't think you're ready," she said. "Come back tomorrow and we'll begin again."

"But—"

"No but," Diana said firmly. "Go."

My heart sank. Arguing was useless, I could see that. But it didn't stop my cheeks from burning. I walked past her, my head high, and had my hand on the doorknob when I heard the slight rustle of her dress and then an almost imperceptible grunt.

I said the word and made the gesture as I swung around

to face her. A rock stopped only inches from my head, hung in the air a moment, then fell to the ground.

I stared at the rock lying near my feet, then laughed. "You're a bit sly, aren't you?"

"Not half so sly as the gremhahn will be," she said.

~

*T*hat night I made a list of the spells I thought I'd need. I brought the list with me when I went to Diana's the next day.

"How are you feeling?" she asked as I settled on the lion's-claw sofa in her front parlor.

"Fine." She'd never asked about my health before and it seemed odd for her to do it now. "Oh," I said. "Because of Mother, that magic made her ill."

"You'll need to watch out for that, Cassie. Your mother didn't see it coming and it overtook her."

A nervous twinge wriggled through my stomach.

You are not your mother, I told myself. *You're young and strong. You can master this.*

"I'll watch out," I said.

Diana raised her eyebrows. "I'll be watching, too. I didn't catch the change with your mother until it was too late. With you, the moment I see that using your magic is having a negative effect, the lessons will stop. Agreed?"

I nodded. "Agreed."

"Good," Diana said. "Now, what do you want to learn today?"

I'd written down the spells to learn in the order I thought I'd need them. But I didn't pick the next spell on the list. I jumped to one near the end.

"I want to know how to break the gremhahn's curse on Mother and the one on me."

Diana gave me a level look. "Why that one now?"

"It's the timing. Last night I wrote out what spells I thought I'd need in the order I thought I'd need them. Capture the gremhahn. Put him under my thrall so he must do what I say. Get Jimmy back. But then I realized—the gremhahn cursed Mother to never see her son again." For a moment, it was impossible to speak. I clenched my hands into loose fists and finished what I had to say. "So the order has to be, capture the sea goblin, put him in thrall, break the curse, then get Jimmy back."

A small smile graced Diana's lips for the tiniest moment, and then was gone. "That's good, Cassie. You're thinking it through." She frowned. "That sort of spell is hard to break. It takes three people."

"You, me, and Mother?" I said.

Diana shook her head. "Your mother may seem fine now, but she's still recovering. You'll have to wait to learn that spell."

I bit back my disappointment and the new worry that sprung up about Mother's health. But Diana said she was recovering. I grabbed that thought and held it, even though Mother had said she'd never do magic again.

"Then a spell to call the gremhahn to me," I said.

"Good," Diana said. "That one's a little harder than the protection spell. Are you ready?"

I nodded and we set to it.

~

New Year's Day brought 1924 into being. Two weeks later, I graduated high school. There were only ten of us for Winter graduation and the ceremony was small. Mother and Diana came. Moira and her parents came, and our old housekeeper, Sophie, as well. The O'Hare's gifted me a signed copy of Sinclair Lewis's *Main Street*, which seemed a bit of an odd choice for them. Mother gave me a gold locket. Inside, one on each side, were photographs of her and of Father. I nearly cried, but Mother took the locket and fastened it around my neck saying, "We will always be with you." There was comfort in that thought.

~

ebruary arrived as a cool day with drizzle. Five days a week, Diana taught me spells and the gestures that went with the spells that needed them. Not all spells did. For some, the word or words were enough. I'd already learned the binding spell from Mother when we'd hunted the sea goblin. Diana taught me her personal spells for finding lost things, so I could eventually find Jimmy. She taught me spells for hiding in plain sight and ways to squeeze or extend time.

"Do you have a spell you'd like to learn today?" Diana asked when I arrived at her house on a Monday morning.

"Not a spell, not right off," I said. "I was wondering about spirit helpers."

Diana raised her eyebrows.

"Like a witch's black cat," I said, only having old folk tales to spark my imagination. That Diana couldn't *offer* spells, that I had to *ask*, was frustrating. I lay awake most nights worrying I was forgetting something that would turn out to be essential—like spirit helpers.

"Cats can be helpers," Diana said, "but not for you. I think, by the way, that you should get a dog."

"A dog is my spirit helper?"

Diana laughed lightly. "No. You should get a dog because I see how lonely you are. Don't think I haven't noticed how you show up early and linger after the lesson is over. You need a companion. People would be better, of course, but you don't seem inclined to make new friends or invite old ones to come around."

I hadn't noticed how isolated I'd kept myself since Father's death and Mother's move to the big house, but Diana was right. Moira and I had gone dancing once since I'd come home to the beach, and of course I called Mother every day, or she called me, and I spent a couple of weekends a month with her, but beyond that people felt like a distraction.

When I wasn't at Diana's, I was home practicing what I'd learned, making sure it was so ingrained that the spells became second nature. But another dog—I wasn't sure about that. When Molly died, it'd broken my heart. In the last year I'd lost my little brother, my dog, and my father. Enough was enough. I didn't want to go through any kind of loss again if I didn't have to.

"So what is my helper, then?" I said.

Diana turned and went toward the kitchen, saying over her shoulder, "Come on. We'll find out."

In the kitchen she took the copper bowl from its place in the cupboard and then brought out a jar of water. This water was clear as glass, not the silty, murky water that had shown me the bow-and-arrow seal.

"We use clear water from a special well near Anza-Borrego for these sorts of things. It has to be pure, with nothing in it to influence the vision. You'll need your own bowl and jars of water eventually."

Her words rolled over me like ice. I hadn't thought beyond breaking the curses on Mother and myself and bringing Jimmy home. Diana seemed to think I would become like her—someone who kept using her magic--and not like Mother, who'd put hers on a dark shelf in the very back of the closet of her life.

What *I* wanted was to go to college, study art and the ocean, and write about where and how they intersected. I wanted to marry and have children. I didn't want to be a magic woman to whom people came for help with their problems. Not that I wouldn't want to help, it was just—

I pushed the worry away. There was time enough to think on all that later. I needed to focus on the here and now. My heart thudded and my nerves jangled as I watched Diana pour the water into the bowl. She pressed her thumb lightly at the spot at the top of my nose, between my eyebrows, then stepped away and said. "Look now and tell me what you see."

I gazed into the bowl. All I saw was water. I stared and stared, waiting for something to appear, but there was nothing. I looked at Diana and shrugged.

Diana pressed her teeth together and made several quick tsking sounds with her tongue—thinking, I thought. Wondering why it didn't work. What was wrong with me that it didn't work?

"It should be sea water," I said suddenly. I didn't know where the idea had come from, but knew I was right. "But filtered clean."

Diana smiled.

I tsked myself. "You knew."

"I knew," Diana said, "but we needed to know if you knew. Learning the words to spells means nothing if you can't tell within yourself what is truly needed at the moment. Your brain might tell you, for instance, that making a small fireball to throw is your best move, but your gut might say this is the time to run. If you can't listen to your inner voice and trust it, you'll make mistakes. The mind is rational and useful, but deep truth is always in the heart. The secret is to get the two in harmony."

She put a funnel in the jar that had held the well water

and carefully poured the water from the bowl back into the jar.

"Another lesson," Diana said. "Never waste your resources."

She screwed the lid back on the jar and returned it to the cupboard. She brought back a jar of seawater that she set on the table in front of me.

"Now," she said, "what will you do with the impurities? The water must be clean for this to work."

"We could strain it through cheesecloth," I said.

Diana said nothing, but she'd given me a look that said that wasn't the sort of answer she was looking for.

"Oh," I said. "I need to do it myself."

I ran a list of spells through my mind. Maybe one to make the sand heavy so it stayed in the bottom of the jar and the clear water could be poured off. Or a gathering spell that might draw the sand and silt together into a solid form, like a rock. Nothing I thought of seemed the right solution.

Then I knew. It wasn't a spell at all that was needed—it was the purest of pure magic, done with the heart alone. I picked up the jar and held it to my chest. I closed my eyes and visualized the silt, sand, tiny sea organisms, whatever might be in the water, disappearing one by one, returned to the ocean from which they'd come, until the sea water was as clear and clean as a baby's first thought.

I *felt* the job was done, but fear slithered in and I didn't open my eyes. What if the seawater was as murky as ever? What if I could cast spells all day long but pure magic was beyond me? How would I ever get Jimmy back if magic was in my head but not my heart?

I had to know, didn't I?

I opened my eyes.

The water in the jar was so clear that it was only the

weight of it that told me something was inside the glass. I grinned, rather proud of myself.

"Pour it in the bowl," Diana said. Impatience rode in her voice and knocked my pride to the floor.

I poured the water in slowly, then set the empty jar on the table. I didn't need to be told again to look into the bowl.

It took no time at all, and I guess I wasn't surprised.

"A fur seal," I said.

"Interesting." Diana rested her chin on her fist. Her eyes were far away. I poured the seawater back into the jar—never waste your resources—while I waited for her to decide whatever it was she was ruminating on. She was taking a while, long enough for me to realize the seawater I'd returned was still crystal clear—not at all the murky water I'd first poured out. I closed my eyes and *thought* the sand, sediment, and bits of whatever had been in the water originally back into the jar, wondering briefly where they had been while they were gone. I opened my eyes and was fairly surprised to see that it had actually worked.

Diana cleared her throat. "I've been thinking and thinking about an object of power for you."

I didn't know what an object of power was, but guessed it was like the compass or Mother's ring—a thing to help me know when I was near my quarry.

"It's all ocean for you. The sea goblin. The shell. The goblin using gulls as his surrogates. The seals that clamored to get your attention at the cove. A seal as your guide animal."

I nodded.

"Well," she said brightly, "there's really only one object that makes sense for you. Hold on a moment while I fetch it."

She returned carrying a thin silver neck chain with a small silver starfish hanging from it. She motioned with her head for me to turn around, and she fastened on the necklace. It hung next to the locket with my parents' portraits inside.

"Never take this off," she said.

I fingered the small starfish. "How does it work?"

"On its own," Diana said. "Which is why you must always wear it. You never know when it will be needed and you want to be sure to have it on when you do."

"What does it do?" I said.

"It's a weapon. If you're lucky, you'll never find out what it does."

I swallowed, thinking things were suddenly moving a little faster than I liked.

ELEVEN

Hermosa Beach, California
March 1924

The sun sank toward the horizon, lighting the clouds pink, orange, blue, and yellow. The tide was out and the ocean calm. I loved the beach in late winter and early spring—the summer tourists not yet descending, the sand stretching on with only the occasional person for as far as I could see. The waves rolled in, their soft melody soothing.

Somewhere out there, my little brother was stuck in a seashell.

I tried the calling spell, feeling the words roll through my lips, listening closely to the sound to hear any imperfections. There was one, maybe.

My heart lurched. I wasn't ready to capture the gremhahn, I knew that—not until Diana and Mother could help me break the curses—but how could I know if I could do it if I didn't do a trial run? I'd call him, and when he came, do what? This had been a stupid thing to do. I needed an undo spell, but I didn't have one. Oh God, I thought, let me fail.

Please let me fail.

Please.

No sea goblin appeared.

I wiped non-existent sweat from my forehead, relieved. Sometimes failure is success.

I turned to walk back to the house and caught sight of a man staring at me. I didn't think the man was a gremhahn disguise. The coincidence would be too deep if I'd failed to call him to me but he was here anyway. I stared back at the stranger, a tactic I'd found usually scared off men who were rude enough to keep their eyes on me.

My breath caught in my throat when I recognized him— the beautiful human. It'd been a while since that night, but I'd have known him even if it had been ten years. No one had any right to be that handsome.

"Please excuse the stare," he said in that voice like honey-butter as he walked up to me, "but have we met? You look familiar."

"We have," I said, taking in the loose cut of his navy-blue trousers, white shirt, and light blue sweater, and the way they fit him. "Very briefly, at Mimi's, downtown. The party broke up because word came the place was about to be raided. You offered my friend and me a ride, but our car was nearby."

"Ah," he said. "I don't remember the incident but I knew I'd seen you before. Do you live around here?"

I felt suddenly wary and I swear the starfish at my throat wiggled slightly. Handsome or not, a lady didn't go around telling strangers where she lived. Not if she were smart.

"No. I live in Wilmington. I'm just here for the day."

"Ah," he said again and doffed the posh flat cap he was wearing. "Well, it was a pleasure to see you again. Have a lovely evening."

He turned and walked south on the beach, in the direction my house lay. I stood a while longer, staring out at the waves, only occasionally sneaking a peek to see if I could still spot him. When he'd gone from my view, I headed home.

~

*D*iana drew her lips together and then let out an angry huff of air when I told her I'd tried to call the sea goblin, just to see if the spell worked, but had failed.

"You can't run before you learn to walk, Cassie," she said. "You're lucky the spell didn't work. What did you think you would do it if did?"

I glanced down at my hands clasped in my lap. "I would have cast a binding spell and captured him in the same burlap bag Mother used. I would have kept him captive until we could work a spell to break the curses on Mother and me and then made him return my brother."

"Three spells," Diana said, "and you so sure that you could do each one correctly when you couldn't even get the first one right. And what on earth made you think you could hold the gremhahn captive for any length of time? Where were you going to put him?"

Heat warmed my cheeks. I was seated on the claw-footed yellow couch in her parlor. I squeezed my folded hands together. "I got ahead of myself."

"Yes, you did."

I'd never heard her voice be so hard and cold. I deserved it, though. She was right and I'd been wrong. I cleared my throat and looked up at her. "I'm very sorry."

"Well, perhaps we should break it into its individual pieces. First, the gathering spell." She glanced around the room. The gathering spell only worked with living things, not objects, so there was nothing in the room for me to bespell.

"Outside," she said and rose from the sofa and headed toward the back door.

I followed her out to the yard.

"My neighbors have a cat," she said. "A Siamese called Ting-a-ling. Call it to you."

I visualized a Siamese cat in my mind and began muttering the spell.

"So I can hear you, Cassie. How will I know if you've got it right if I can't hear the words? Plus, the living thing you're calling won't *hear* it unless it's said clearly."

I touched the starfish and began again, still low but loud enough for Diana to hear. I finished and waited, but no cat appeared.

"Not gown-long-in," Diana said. "Not gown like you wear to a ball. Gown like own with a soft g in front."

I closed my eyes and tried again, carefully pronouncing each word. My eyes flew open when I heard a soft meow at my feet. I clapped my hands, pleased with myself.

Diana didn't give me so much as a small smile. "Now, that sparrow there in the orange tree. Bring it here."

For the rest of the afternoon I fetched two more neighborhood cats, a finch, a large black crow, three earthworms— I failed on earthworm one and Diana made me do it right twice before moving on—and a rather angry raccoon that Diana immediately sent back where it came from.

"Getting tired?" she finally asked, as the sun was sinking quickly westward.

I nodded. My eyes burned, my head ached, and my spine had curved into a slump. I'd been concentrating hard for hours. I was exhausted, hungry, and ready to go home.

"One more," she said. "I have a nephew who lives in Gardena." She reached into her pocket and drew out a photograph. I was pretty sure Diana didn't carry his photo in her pocket at all times and wondered if she'd somehow known of my failure with the goblin and what today's lesson would be, or if she'd done some spell I'd completely missed that put the photo in her pocket. "Bring him to us."

"Won't he mind being snatched away from whatever he's doing?" I said.

"No," she said. "I phoned him."

"When?"

Diana smiled slightly. "I have my secrets, Cassie. Lessons you are years away from learning."

Was that so? I thought. Well, watch this. I spoke the spell loudly and clearly and was not at all surprised when Diana's nephew—a rangy boy, younger than me, with wild, curly yellow hair—materialized in the backyard.

"How was it?" Diana asked her nephew.

"A bit bumpy," he said, "but effective enough."

He peered at me. "Why do you wear your hair pulled back like an old school marm?"

The heat of embarrassment stung my cheeks. Nineteen years old and I looked to this boy like an old woman with my hair pulled into a tight bun. Anger burned in my chest at the sea goblin and at the stars that reminded me each morning as I pinned up my hair of the price Mother, Jimmy, and I would pay if I failed at the task I'd set for myself.

Diana chuffed the side of his head lightly. "Does your mother teach you manners or not?"

The boy shrugged. "Sorry," he muttered in my direction. "None of my business."

"Does your aunt often summon you this way?" I asked, to show I wasn't angry with him and to turn the conversation.

He nodded and grinned. "Auntie Di is a teacher, so I help out with student spell-castings when she needs me. She's my teacher, too. I get extra lessons in return for playing the guinea pig."

"Andrew has been training in spell-craft since he was seven. He'll make a fine mage one of these days."

I judged Andrew to be fourteen or so now. Seven years he'd been training. Would it take me seven years before I could bring Jimmy back? I couldn't bear that.

Andrew gave his aunt a hug. Diana kissed his cheek. She muttered something and made a swirling motion with her hand, and the nephew was gone.

She dusted her hands together. "All right. That's enough for today. Tomorrow at ten."

"I have something I need to do in the morning. Can we make it noon?"

Diana sent me a harsh look but said, "Noon will be fine."

~

As soon as I finished breakfast I took the Red Car to the dog pound in Carson. Part of me was hesitant to love a dog again, but I knew that a heart that didn't love shriveled and died. Getting a dog would set two lives on a happier road—mine and its.

The pound was as sad and depressing as I'd thought it would be—and loud with dogs barking. I walked through the kennels peering into every cage, some dogs barking at me, some standing, their tails wagging hopefully, and others cowering in the back as if afraid every moment that a blow would fall on them. Just when I thought I'd never be able to choose only one, I spied a medium-sized yellow dog with one ear that went up and one that flopped over, and I knew. This was my dog.

"She's a girl but we call her Scout," the pound worker said. "Like the motorcycle."

I looked at him blankly.

"The Indian Motorcycle Company, do you know it? No? They make a model called the Scout. Seems to fit her."

I continued my blank stare.

"Because she's really fast," the man said, emphasizing the last word. "She's got some Labrador retriever in her, obviously, and who knows what else. She's small for a Lab. Probably won't get bigger than forty, fifty pounds."

"I'll take her," I said.

The man tied a rope around the yellow dog's neck, brought her out of the cage, and handed the rope to me. We went up front so I could complete the paperwork and pay the fee. Scout had trotted up right beside me and sat calmly at my side while I took care of the business side of the transaction.

"Could you call a taxi, please," I asked the man. "Be sure to mention I'll have a dog with me."

"Cabbies all know this address," he said. "They're used to happy people having dogs with them, or people without dogs, with glum faces or tears streaking their cheeks."

I reached down and scratched Scout behind the ears. I'd be one of the happy ones.

❧

I'd gone to the pound so early that after we returned home I still had an hour before I needed to be at Diana's.

"What do you think, Scout," I said, addressing the dog. "Shall we have a walk on the beach?"

Scout cocked her head and listened, her tail wagging slowly, puzzling out the meanings of the words, I supposed.

I changed the rope to Molly's old collar—it was too big

and I had to punch a new hole for the buckle with a knife—and Molly's leash, and we headed for the sand.

We walked along the shore. Scout was a dream on the leash, trotting at my heels, her head swiveling this way and that, taking it all in. I supposed she'd never seen the ocean before.

I thought how foolish I'd been to try to call the sea goblin to me. Diana had shown me how much more I needed to learn before I tried anything like that again. Next time I would be completely ready.

"A long way from home to be walking your dog," a voice like melted honey-butter said next to me.

I swung my head and looked at the owner of the voice—that beautiful human again.

He smiled. "If you live in Wilmington, seems there would be closer places for a walk."

I laughed under my breath. I'd been caught out in my lie and we both knew it.

"I live a ways down the Strand," I said, watching Scout sniff at the man's pant leg. Dogs seem to know instinctively if someone is a good person or not, and I was curious what Scout would make of him. She seemed a bit confused as she sniffed, then looked to the ocean, then sniffed him again. In the end, she must have decided he was all right, because she didn't object when he sank down over his ankles and scratched her under the chin.

"Her name is Scout," I said.

"Like the motorcycle?"

It must be a male thing, I decided. All males instinctively knew the names of motorcycles, a thing about which I knew absolutely nothing.

"Because she's fast," I said, and glanced at my watch. Eleven thirty. I needed to turn back now and take Scout home and get her settled if I was going to arrive at Diana's at noon.

"It was nice to meet you again," I said and started to walk away.

"Would it seem very forward of me to ask to walk with you a bit?" He bowed slightly when I turned back toward him. "Paxton Yeager, Pax, at your service."

He'd introduced himself at Mimi's and I'd remembered his name. Who could forget the name of someone who looked like he did?

"Oh," I said, realizing he meant for me to introduce myself in return. "Cassie Goodlight."

"A pleasure," he said. "You have a lovely name. Goodlight is unusual."

I laughed lightly. "Family lore is that when Great-Grand-father came from France, the only English he knew was hello, goodbye, please, thank you, good morning, and good night. After handing over his papers at Ellis Island, when the clerk asked his name, Great Grand-Pere thought he was being told to go on through, so he said what he believed was proper at parting—he said, "Good night." The clerk didn't even get it correct though, writing down Good*light*. Which is how we went from being DuPont to the name we have now.

"Or I could be a descendent of the famous Indian princess Morning-Star Goodlight of the Swirling Waters tribe."

I was babbling. Something about Paxton Yeager made me wary and giddy in the same instant. I abruptly shut up.

Pax smiled. "A lovely name, however you came by it."

"Thank you." I turned and walked toward the house.

He didn't try to make further conversation as we made our way, first by the shore and then across the sand and then to the concrete Strand and finally to my house. I appreciated his silence, especially after my inane prattle about my last name. I was never one of those girls who could giggle and bat their eyelashes at any boy who came near. Moira often said I'd never get a boyfriend, much less a husband, if I didn't learn how to, in her words, flirt and listen.

"Men love to talk and love an appreciative audience even more," she'd said.

A small lump formed in my throat. There'd be no boyfriends and certainly no husband for me if I couldn't break the sea goblin's curse.

~

I spent every weekday at Diana's perfecting my spells—not only the ones I'd identified as important, but more that Diana said I needed. I didn't know when I'd crossed the invisible border that allowed Diana to suggest spells, but one day she simply did, as if she had been doing so all along. I'd shot her a look of curiosity, but had gotten the distinct feeling I shouldn't actually mention the change. Evidently there were rules to this magic business that Diana followed but I was not to be privileged to know. That was fine with me, so long as I broke the curse on Mother and got Jimmy back.

In the evenings Scout and I went for walks. I felt guilty leaving her at home alone all day and made up for it with long walks on the beach. My back door had a smaller swinging door in it for her to go in and out to the backyard, but home alone was home alone—except that I loved being home by myself, so maybe Scout didn't mind it, either.

She was good about walking on the leash, never pulling, though she'd eye the birds on the sand and I knew she wanted to chase them.

"Wait a minute," I said one evening, and dropped down beside her to unhook her leash. There were a few people out enjoying the last of the day, but not so many that I thought anyone would mind a loose dog. Scout sat in the sand and looked at me.

"You poor thing," I said. "What life did you have before this that you don't know how to run free?" I shooed her with my hands. "Go! Run!"

I swear she smiled and then jumped up and ran at a small flock of seagulls resting one-legged on the sand. The birds rose into the air as Scout came near them.

Good, I thought. Fly off, seagulls, and tell your goblin master there will be no peace as long as Cassie and Scout patrol the sand.

Scout ran down to the shore and along the water's edge, barking at something only she could see. I shaded my eyes, trying to determine what she was barking at, and spied a lone seal swimming parallel to Scout's run on the shore. The seal swam away from me, toward the cliffs of Palos Verde. Scout ran alongside—the man at the pound had been right; she was very fast—until she was far enough away that worry tightened my chest.

"Scout! Scout!" I called, running down the beach after her. I ran until I was out of breath and had to stop. I bent over, breathing hard. What if Scout chased the seal into the water and a wave knocked her down? What if she was caught in a riptide? If she left the shore and ran up to the Strand and then into some street, she'd never find her way home.

When I'd caught enough breath to finally straighten up again, my heart soared to see Scout still running along where the seal swam, but heading my direction. When she reached me, the seal dove under the water and disappeared.

"Thanks for bringing my dog back," I said, as if the seal could hear me. After all, wasn't the seal my spirit animal?

*S*cout was snoring lightly at the end of my bed. I stared into the dark, thinking about Jimmy. It'd been seven months since he disappeared and three months since I'd first gone to the finder woman to learn just enough spell-craft to bring my brother home. How much longer could Mother stand not having Jimmy back? How much longer could I?

TWELVE

Hermosa Beach, California
April 1924

The moment Diana let me into her house, in the foyer, before we'd even gone into the parlor, I said, "I need an answer from you. When will I be ready to go after the sea goblin, break the curses, and save my brother?"

Diana gave me a level stare. "When do you think you'll be ready?"

I squared my shoulders. "I'm ready now. I know every spell I'll need by heart. I've proved that I can do them, and that they work. I know more than I'll need to capture the gremhahn and rescue Jimmy. All this extra rigmarole, knowing how to throw fire balls or levitate, it's unnecessary. Even though I asked to learn those things, it's wasting time. Jimmy is stuck in that shell." I drew myself up as tall as I could. I was taller than Diana on any day. Now I wanted to tower over her. I wanted her to see how strong I was.

"I know how to walk, Diana. I'm ready to run."

"The same way you were *ready* before when you couldn't even call the sea goblin to you?" she said.

My cheeks flamed. It was true I'd jumped too soon then, but I knew so much more now. I'd thought through every step, every situation I could conceive of, and asked Diana for a spell to turn every one of those situations to my advantage. If the binding spell didn't work, what secondary spell would accomplish the same thing? If the sea goblin didn't come in human form, what spell would change him to it? Except for needing three to break the curses, I was as prepared as I ever would be.

"Have you found your ally yet?" she asked quietly.

I folded a little. "You never said I needed an ally."

"So, no," she said. "You haven't."

I cleared my throat, buying a little time before answering. Was it sheer arrogance that made me feel ready? I didn't think so.

"I guess not," I said a bit haughtily. "A human ally, or something like the seal?"

"If you don't know the answer to that, you certainly are not ready to seek the goblin."

You're wrong, I thought. *I am ready. I'm going to do it.*

Judging by the way Diana's mouth pinched, she knew exactly what I'd been thinking. Must have been the set of my face and body.

Or mind reading? Could she teach me a spell that would let me read the goblin's intentions? What if the goblin could read mine? Clearly I *hadn't* thought of every eventuality yet.

"Go home, Cassie," Diana said. "Come back when you're ready to learn."

"But—" I said, afraid now that she'd not let me come back.

She shook her head. "Just go home."

Fury pounded through me. I was ready. I was.

"Cassie," she said softly, "be careful of yourself."

What did that mean? Did she think I was like Mother, that magic was unhinging me?

Was magic unhinging me?

Fatigue hit me suddenly. All these months, all the worry—it'd worn me out. I wasn't unhinged, I was exhausted. Diana saw that. Saw it before I had, certainly.

I turned and went out the door and down the walk. Scout would be glad to see me. A long nap and a walk on the sand —that's what I needed. And maybe we'd run into Pax on the beach.

That thought surprised me, but really, when I considered it, it shouldn't have. Paxton Yeager had come into my mind more than a few times lately.

I reached up under my hat and touched one of the stars in my hair. *No romance for you, Cassie Goodlight. Not unless you break the curses. If they can be broken.*

Exhausted or not, undoing Mother's curse and saving Jimmy were what mattered. I'd find a way to make Diana understand that. A way to make her stop throwing road-blocks in my path. Maybe find a workaround so I could force the gremhahn myself to unhex Mother. I would bring Jimmy home.

$\approx$

*I*t seemed prudent to stay away from Diana for a few days—let it seem I was contemplating all she'd said to me. And in truth, I'd slept through most of my first day off and it had helped. I'd also thought of a few more things I probably should know before I took on the gremhahn, and that revelation made me consider that I'd never think of everything, and would never be ready.

On Wednesdays I did my shopping. It seemed to me that fewer people chose that day, and I liked a less-crowded store. I was walking north on the Strand, up to Santa Fe Avenue, the wicker picnic basket I used to carry groceries over my arm, when I saw Pax come out of the Berth Hotel. The two-story whitewashed stucco building, with its large windows facing the beach, accommodated the growing number of visitors coming from as far away as other states now for vacation.

Pax stood a moment, looking first one way and then the other, up and down the Strand. His hair was wet, I thought, so he must have just come from a bath. I waved when I caught his eye. He smiled and walked toward me.

My stomach suddenly clenched and an odd fluttery feeling ran through me.

"Good morning, Miss Goodlight," he said in that honey-butter voice of his, and doffed the felt hat he wore. He spied the basket over my arm. "On your way to a picnic?"

"Shopping," I said. "There's a grocery around the corner on Santa Fe. I buy my victuals there."

He nodded as if storing the information away for later. "Mrs. Berth sets a good table, but I'm a bit tired of the same thing every day. I'm on my way to lunch out. I hope I'm not being too forward, but would you have time to join me?"

"I've eaten," I said, "but a cup of tea would be lovely. It's chilly this morning."

That odd fluttery feeling sped through me again as he offered his arm and I took it. I felt the starfish at my throat wriggle slightly and worried first that Pax might see it move, and then that I was simply imagining things and needed to get a firmer grip on myself.

We walked up Santa Fe Avenue to Kerwin's Bakery and Lunch Room. Inside the red brick building, the two oldest

Kerwin boys sat coloring at a table near the kitchen. Baby Ted lay in a basinet next to the table. The scents of fresh-baked bread and cookies were heavenly. I was a little sorry I'd already eaten.

When our order came, Pax ate his meal with good manners but also with gusto. I mostly stirred my tea and asked, "What sort of work do you do?"

Pax set down his fork. "I'm teaching a course on folklore at the University of Southern California." He laughed under his breath. "It's not very popular, I'm sorry to say. I doubt I'll be invited to stay on for the next session."

My attention was piqued by his specialty, but what I asked was, "Aren't you a little young to be a professor?"

He half-shrugged. "Perhaps."

I smiled. "Are you a prodigy of some sort?"

"I wouldn't say prodigy—more impatient than anything. I finished my master's degree at nineteen. My book, *English, Scottish, and Irish Folklore in the United States*, gave me a bit of notoriety. Surprised me, to tell you the truth. It's rather academic for the casual reader, but it was enough to get me invited to this teaching position."

I cleared my throat, my mind racing. "Have you ever heard of a gremhahn?"

He nodded. "Is your family Irish? The story of the gremhahn is fairly common in Irish folklore."

"Someone in town told me the story. I suppose she might be Irish, though she doesn't have an accent. I went to the library downtown to learn more. One book said the gremhahn steals children and eats them." I paused a moment. I hadn't read any versions that told the tale the way it had happened to Jimmy, but I wanted to see Pax's reaction. "Another book said that a stolen child could be kept in a seashell."

Pax raised his eyebrows. "I've never heard either of those versions of the tale. I'd like to talk to your friend. In all the stories I've heard, the gremhahn—there's only one, you know, not like giants, fairies, or ogres. The gremhahn doesn't eat the children it steals. It turns them into seals. The selkies —do you know about the selkies?"

My heart beat like a wild horse racing in my chest. *The seals are your friends*, the Japanese man had said. Was one of them also my brother?

"Yes," I said, keeping my voice even. "My mother told me about selkies."

"The selkies," Pax said, "care for the children turned to seals and try to find their families so they can be returned. There's a time limit. If a child isn't returned within a year, he or she remains a seal."

My heart pounded so hard I thought it might break out of my chest. Jimmy had disappeared last July 17. Three more months and he would stay a seal forever, if Pax were right.

My mind twisted in so many directions at once, it was hard to grab a single thought and see it through. I wanted to move—to walk and think. Four months left in which to learn everything I needed to know, to break the curses on Mother and myself, to save Jimmy from the sea goblin.

"Thank you for the tea," I said. "I should be on my way."

"Of course," Pax said, rising from his chair.

He gave me a piercing look as he stood, and I wished I could see into his mind, to what he was thinking. I wished I didn't feel as though he could see into me quite clearly.

~

I lit the lantern to provide more light than the sliver of moon offered. Scout darted ahead, her head high, apparently hearing something beyond the fence at the east end of the property. An alley ran behind there, but the fence was seven feet high, so I couldn't see what might have caught her attention. I'd not noticed it before, but realized at that moment that Father had highly prized privacy.

Scout sniffed along the edge of the fence, her hackles raised. I watched her with wary eyes. I'd long since asked Diana for a spell of protection that I'd cast over my house and Mother's. I trusted it worked, but unless I saw the goblin try to breach it and fail, I couldn't know for sure. Scout gave a last, loud snuff at the fence, and the hair at the back of her neck went down. She trotted back to me, evidently having decided that whoever or whatever was moving down the alley posed no threat. I cast another protection spell over the house and yard anyway, visualizing layer upon layer of invisible shield, just to be on the safe side.

Diana insisted Mother still wasn't ready to help with the curse breaking. I didn't want to ask Mother myself. It wouldn't matter that she'd said she wanted nothing more to do with magic. I knew she'd try to help, whether she was ready or not. I also knew Jimmy's time was running out. I wasn't sure why I took Pax at his word that the gremhahn had lied about Jimmy being in the shell, that my brother was now a seal and would remain one if we didn't get him back before his year was up, but I did.

Which meant, now that I thought about it, that the binding spell Mother cast on the gremhahn hadn't worked if he could lie. What good was a spell that wouldn't work? Maybe Mother hadn't done it exactly right. Maybe she'd only partially enchanted him, so that some of what he said was truth and some a lie.

Which meant I had to be perfect with my spells. Which meant practice and more practice.

I didn't want to call anything obvious, especially if people were going to be walking by my fence, even if it was night. A flock of crows suddenly descending on my yard or the neighborhood cats disappearing and then reappearing here might be a little too noticeable. I closed my eyes and visualized a couple of gophers popping their heads out of their holes. It's likely Scout would go for them, but I wouldn't bind the animals and they could hie back into their dens quicker than Scout could get them. Besides, how many gophers could live in my yard? Not that many.

I opened my eyes and pronounced the calling spell.

The yard was instantly overrun with gophers—dozens of them scurrying this way and that. Scout was barking and chasing after first one, then another. One ran straight toward me and I jumped to avoid it. These weren't just the gophers from my yard—those dove quickly back into their dens—but probably half the gophers in Hermosa. I quickly sent them back whence they'd come.

Scout padded up next to me and sniffed at my leg. I knelt beside her and scratched behind her ears. My pulse was hammering. I couldn't make mistakes like this when the day came to save Jimmy.

"It's a good thing there's only one sea goblin," I said to her. "If there were more, I'd likely wind up calling them all at once."

She licked my cheek, giving me a dog kiss. Funny how something that simple made me feel much better. I kissed her back on the top of her head.

"What shall we try next?" I said, pulling myself to my feet. "How about opossums? Have you ever seen a 'possum? So ugly they are cute. But let's not bring a mob this time. One might do."

I cast the spell. The moment the last word left my mouth, Scout bolted for the back gate, barking, but wagging her tail in the same happy way she did when I came home. Had I drawn the possum to the alley rather than my yard? That was worrisome.

I followed Scout to the back gate that opened onto the alley, cracked it open enough for me to see, my body angled so Scout couldn't run out. She pushed at my legs trying to get through, distracting me, so I didn't see Pax for a moment.

"Good evening," he said, tipping his fedora to me. He was dressed casually but well, in a new-style loose-fitting dark navy suit. The slightly nipped-in waist of the jacket drew attention to his broad shoulders.

Magic was still zinging through me, and I suppose it was surprise at seeing him that made me demand, "What are you doing here?"

Pax actually smiled at my harsh tone.

"Passing by," he said. "I heard there was a good Italian place on Second Street. I was on my way there. Would you care to join me?"

I drew in a breath and pulled myself together.

"I have dinner cooking on the stove," I said, "but thank you for the offer. Perhaps another time."

Pax dipped his head but lingered.

"There's plenty," I said, rather surprised I was inviting someone who was mostly a stranger into my home. "If you like shepherd's pie."

"One of my favorites," he said in that honeyed voice.

Scout had switched her attention from Pax to something behind me.

Pax followed her with his eyes. "You seem to have some critters in your yard."

I swung around and saw Scout slowly stalking a possum family. I'd seen her stalk before, her head down, taking slow, small steps. In a moment, she'd bolt for them. She was fast. She could catch the mother or one of the babies if it fell off her back. Without thinking, I said the spell to return them from wherever they'd come from.

"Whoa," Pax said, and I swung back to face him.

He was looking at me as if I'd suddenly sprouted an extra arm or my hair had turned to grass.

"You're a witch."

THIRTEEN

Hermosa Beach, California
April 1924

"*M*age," I said, relieved somehow to have it out in the open.

Pax nodded slightly, acknowledging my words.

"Witches are born with their magic fully formed," I said, repeating something Diana had said. "A mage learns to cultivate and grow innate talent."

A slight smile curved his lips, but I didn't feel he was humoring me. It was more like he was pleased.

The alarm I'd set to go off when the pie was finished dinged in the kitchen. "Shall we go in?"

I set the table, lit the candles, and brought out the shepherd's pie I'd planned on eating for the next few days, along with two cups of tea. I wanted to know what he thought about my announcement, but didn't ask. It felt comfortable having him in the house. Maybe I didn't want to know he was secretly laughing, or thought I was a little crazy, or saw me as a story to be collected for his next book.

Mother had taught me to cook starting when I was about seven. I was pretty good at it, to judge by what others had said. Pax was clearly enjoying the meal, and I didn't think it was from good manners alone.

"You're my first dinner guest since the house became mine," I said.

Pax set down his glass and smiled. "I'm honored." He took another bite of pie. When he'd swallowed he said, "So, what prompted you to want to learn magic?"

I fiddled with my fork. I could say, what? *I'd always wanted to learn.* Or maybe: *It's a hobby.* That didn't sound right. Who takes up real spell-craft as a hobby?

"Two years ago, my brother was stolen by the gremhahn," I said. "I aim to get him back. A woman is teaching me too use the magic I was born with so I can do that."

I held my breath, waiting to see and hear Pax's response. He simply nodded and took another bite of pie.

"You don't seem to find my explanation odd," I said.

He finished his last bite and wiped his mouth with a linen napkin. "I've seen more than a few things that couldn't be explained. I've learned not to be a skeptic."

"Like what?" I asked.

"Mermaids," Pax said. "And selkies."

I couldn't tell if he was teasing or not. He smiled slowly. I pursed my lips. He was kidding.

"What do you think?" he said. "Can I meet this friend of yours who knows about the gremhahn?"

I hesitated. I wasn't sure if it was acceptable to bring a stranger to Diana's home. But Mother and I were strangers to her when we'd first appeared on her doorstep, and Diana never had hidden her abilities. Everyone in town knew she was magical.

"I don't think she'd mind. Can you come tomorrow morning at ten?"

"I'll be here," he said. "Do you walk or drive there?"

"Walk," I said. "It's up a rather steep hill. Are you used to walking hills?"

"I can manage," he said, "but if you don't mind, I'll bring my car and drive us."

$\sim$

*T*he next day, a little before ten, I fastened on a yellow broad-brimmed hat that complimented the blue tunic and skirt set I wore. The tunic had a button-on cape, good for a cool morning like this one. Needing an extra boost of daring, I pulled on canary yellow gloves. Anyone who would wear gloves like these must be bold, I told myself.

Was I too bold, allowing Pax to come with me to Diana's? I didn't think so. I truly didn't think she'd mind.

But perhaps I'd been foolhardy. I barely knew the man and yet was about to climb into his car and take him to meet someone magical. Moira wouldn't have thought twice about it. She'd have swung into the passenger seat ready for adventure.

Since the war's end and the coming of prohibition, women were becoming increasingly bold in their demands to live their lives as they chose, far beyond the right to wear trousers. We had the vote now, and I would proudly cast my ballet as soon as I was twenty-one and eligible.

Wasn't I a bit bold myself, choosing to live at the beach independent of a parent, guardian, or even a friend? And what of my lessons with Diana? I'd ignored Mother's words that my finding Jimmy would come naturally and taken a more aggressive path. Compared to that decision, accepting a ride from a near stranger was nothing.

Perhaps I'd chosen the yellow gloves not to give me courage but as a sign of the woman I had become.

I called out to Scout, who was rooting around in the bedroom for something, likely a misplaced toy. She trotted down the stairs with her favorite toy—a stuffed duck—in her mouth, dropped it at my feet and gave me a crestfallen look. I scratched her ears.

"I won't be gone long. When I get back, we'll go for a nice run on the beach."

She didn't look mollified, but she picked up her duck and took it out the back door.

At the sound of a knock, I opened the front door to find Pax waiting. He wore a brown tweed suit—again in the new style, with wide shoulders and loose pants. I'd seen one or two of the fellows at Mimi's dressed this way, but they hadn't worn their clothes with half the cleverness Pax did. My canary yellow gloves seemed to fit right in.

He held out a rectangular box sheathed in blue paper. "I think I missed your birthday."

I smiled and took the box. "Last week. March 21st."

"Vernal equinox," he said. "Good birthday for a mage."

"Clever of my mother to plan it that way," I said.

He smiled and glanced at the package in my hands. "Open it."

Inside was his book.

"I hope it doesn't seem vain to give you my own book, but I thought you might like to have one at home," he said. "Save you a trip to the library should you ever want to learn more about the legends."

I opened the cover. He'd inscribed it *To Cassie, a woman of intelligence, curiosity, and magic.*

My cheeks grew warm. "Thank you. I'll treasure it."

"My car is around back—parked in the alley," he said, and offered his arm. "Shall we go?"

I drew in a breath when I saw his car—a blood red Hemmings Speedster with a long bonnet and butter cream interior. It was a good thing my hair was pinned up and I'd worn a hat with ribbons to tie under my chin. Pax opened the passenger-side door for me. I stepped onto the running board and slid in as gracefully as I could. He went around to the driver's side, climbed in himself, and started the vehicle.

The car roared to life like a large animal proclaiming its presence. We sped up the alley toward Santa Fe Avenue. Even with the ribbons tied, I had to hold down my hat with my hand. We drove up Santa Fe to the Roosevelt Highway, Pax expertly weaving the car in and out of the light traffic. Everyone we passed seemed to stare, though I couldn't tell whether it was the car or Pax that entranced them.

Diana met us at the door. Likely she'd heard the car coming up the hill. She opened her arms and gave me a quick hug, but narrowed her eyes at Pax. Maybe she didn't approve of his choice of suits or cars.

"Paxton Yeager," he said, extending his hand. "A friend of Cassie's.

"He teaches folklore at USC," I quickly added, hoping that would make him seem more legitimate somehow.

"Your mother is here," Diana said, taking his hand as briefly as was possible and still be polite, then ignoring Pax as she swept us into the house.

I introduced my mother to Pax. She, at least, seemed to find him acceptable. Diana, though, kept giving him harsh looks.

"I'll put on the kettle," she said as I settled on the yellow claw-foot couch next to Mother.

"Please let me help," Pax said and strode off toward the kitchen as though he knew the way from long familiarity.

Mother turned to me, her eyes as bright as a bird's. "Who is this Paxton?"

I felt an unexpected heat rising in my cheeks. "We met on the beach when I was walking Scout," I said. "He teaches folklore and was interested in meeting Diana. I didn't think she'd mind, but she doesn't seem very happy he's here."

Mother patted my hand. "Diana is very fond of you. She's looking out for your best interests."

They came back through the door then—Diana with a tray of petit fours, Pax with the heavier pewter tea tray. Whatever tension Diana had felt seemed to be gone.

When we were all settled in the parlor, I said, "Pax told me something interesting the other day about children taken by the gremhahn."

I'd worried that Mother would be unhappy at my bringing up this subject, but she leaned forward, interested.

"He said that in the folk stories he'd heard, the sea goblin turns the stolen children into seals. He said the selkies watch over the transformed children and try to reunite them with their families. I think the goblin saying Jimmy was in the seashell was a trick."

Which shouldn't have been possible. The gremhahn, under Mother's binding spell, should have been compelled to tell only the truth. Either Mother had gotten the spell wrong or the spell itself didn't work and the goblin had tricked us, pretending to be bound when he wasn't. Either way, it was a worry.

Mother narrowed her eyes and looked at Pax. Likely she was having thoughts similar to my own. Likely she was also thinking about the ramifications of Paxton's version of things.

"Seals and selkies," she said. "Only in stories, or is it true?"

Pax seemed to think over the question. I dug my nails lightly into the heel of my palm. He'd say it was only stories, folktales. He'd teased me, saying he'd seen mermaids and selkies, but of course he hadn't. He couldn't know the gremhahn was real, no matter what I'd told him. He'd douse Mother's brief flare of hope.

"I would say," Pax said, "and most experts in my field would say, that there's truth behind every folktale."

Mother considered that. "How much truth would you say lies in your tale of the gremhahn?"

"*If* the gremhahn were real, then my version would be one hundred percent accurate."

I cleared my throat. "Pax told me something else—that the stolen child only has a year in which to be transformed back into a human. After that, he'll be a seal forever."

My words hit mother hard and she gasped.

"Which means," I said, plowing on, "we have three months left to save Jimmy."

My eyes were on Diana as I spoke. Her face was calm, and I thought that she'd known this all along. Anger flamed in my chest. If she knew, why had she kept putting off a rescue attempt?

"Yes," Diana said. "We must make sure you are completely ready before then."

I wanted to ask about breaking the curses, the spell that took three, but Mother seemed too upset for me to broach it now. Ready or not, healthy or not, she'd agree to anything to get her son back.

Diana said, "We'll go over each of the spells, to be sure you have them right. We'll start with the binding spell."

A spell that, if Pax was right, hadn't worked on the gremhahn for Mother. What if it didn't work when I tried it either?

"What's the binding spell?" Pax asked. "What does it do?"

Diana shrugged. "As it sounds. It binds the spellbound to the spell caster."

Pax threw me a smile. "She can cast it on me," he said, which took me aback. "It would be an interesting experience and I assume it can be undone."

Diana arched her eyebrows and shook her head. "Magic

isn't something to be played with. Audrey will be the focus of the spell. Since they are already bound as mother and daughter, there can be no harm done."

I glanced at Mother. Her hands were folded calmly in her lap and her face had a determined set.

"You're not worried?" I said to her. "What if something goes wrong with the spell?"

"It won't," Mother said. "I have complete confidence in you."

I hoped that confidence wasn't misplaced. I looked at Diana. "Are we going to do it right here, in the parlor?"

Diana nodded. I began the spell.

Mother let out a yelp and began shivering uncontrollably.

I shut off the words and grabbed her hands. They were ice cold and shaking as if she'd suddenly developed palsy. Diana said something while she swirled her hands in arcs that began out from her sides and ended in front of her chest. Mother stopped shivering at once—the spell broken.

"Are you all right?" I asked, my voice quivering.

She stared at me blankly a moment, then the light switched on in her eyes.

"I'm fine. What happened?"

"I made a mistake," I said. "I'm sorry. I did something wrong in the spell. You were shaking hard."

Mother pursed her lips. "I don't remember." She put her hand on my cheek. "No need for you to be upset. No harm done."

"Are you sure?" I said.

She nodded. "I'm fine, Cassie. Truly."

I hoped no harm had been done.

I looked over at Diana. "What did I do wrong?" I thought that Diana had been right—Mother wasn't ready for magic. And Jimmy was running out of time.

The finder woman tucked a strand of loose hair behind her ear. "You had two words reversed."

She walked over to a small writing desk in the corner. "I'm going to write the spell down again and I want you to not attempt it or any other enchantment until both you and I are sure you can do them properly."

She didn't have to worry about that. If it weren't for Jimmy, I'd never try magic again after what had happened.

What had Pax made of all this? Diana? Magic? Mother shaking? He was a hard man to read.

Diana handed me the paper, but she didn't sit again. It was clear she was drawing the visit to a close.

We said goodbye and Mother walked us to the door.

Just outside, she drew me aside as Pax walked on toward the car.

"Your young man seems quite nice," she said. "Perhaps you'd like to bring him to dinner sometime."

I threw my arms around her and hugged her close. "I'm so sorry."

"I'm fine, Cassie," she said, emphasizing the *fine*. "Go with your young man now. I'll talk to you soon."

Pax wasn't my young man. No one would ever be my young man if I couldn't break the curses.

I hugged her again and got in when he held the car door open.

What an idiot I was. I'd thought I was ready to take on the sea goblin when I couldn't get even the simplest spell right. I barely noticed when Pax pulled into the alley behind my house, got out, came around and opened the passenger door for me. I tried to snap myself into some sort of conversation, to at least thank him for driving me, but no words could escape the dark thoughts filling my mind.

At the door, Pax drew a small pad of paper and a pen

from inside his suit jacket. He wrote something down and held it out to me.

"This is the telephone number where I'm staying. It seems you need some time to yourself now. Call if you'd like company, or someone to walk the dog with you."

I took the paper and nodded. I didn't know why I did it, but I rose up on my toes and kissed his cheek.

FOURTEEN

Hermosa Beach, California
June 1924

*M*y tired eyes burned from staring at the paper I held. I'd stared at it so hard and for so long that I was half surprised it hadn't burst into flames. My throat was scratchy from reciting the spells Diana had written for me. I wasn't going to mess up again. The next time I met the sea goblin, I'd be ready.

But if I made myself recite the enchantments one more time, I might scream.

I let out a long sigh and set the paper on the kitchen table, then picked up the phone and called Moira.

"What are you doing tonight?" I said.

Her voice dropped to a whisper. "I'm trying to get out of playing dominos for hours and hours with old Uncle Chester. Can you save me?"

"Let's go dancing," I said.

I could practically hear Moira's eyes light up and a grin cross her mouth.

"I just need to dress," she said. "I'll pick you up in two hours." There was a pause, and again I could almost hear the gears moving in Moira's head. Her voice moved up to a normal tone. "Oh, Cassie. I'm so sorry. Let me ask my mother. I'm sure she won't mind if I come over for a while."

Whatever lie Moira had concocted to tell her mother was nothing I wanted to know. I didn't approve of lying to one's parents, but Moira was a bit of a wild child that way, likely because her parents held her leash so loosely, due to her nearly dying from Spanish Flu. Sometimes you have to accept your friends as they are, not as you'd prefer them to be.

I chose a flowing red silk dress with gold trim—perfect for dancing—red t-strap shoes, long white gloves, and a red cloche hat. I checked my reflection in the mirror. The dress fit well and the color made me happy. My fingers touched a star as I adjusted my hat. A tight knot formed in my stomach.

I shook it off. It wasn't romance or love I was after tonight. These damn stars would be gone soon anyway—I'd see to that. The gremhahn would very much regret the day he'd come to our door. I gave my reflection a little salute and said, "Go have fun, Cassie. You deserve it."

Moira picked me up in the dark-green Italian sports car her parents had given her for her nineteenth birthday. It already had a ding in the fender from her sometimes enthusiastic driving. Moira refused to have it repaired, calling it a "battle scar."

"Mimi's again?" she asked.

"It'll do," I said, and smiled.

Mimi's was just as packed and noisy as the last time I'd been there. The air was thick with cigarette smoke and the faintly mixed scent of perfume, aftershave, and sweat. We looked around for an empty table, but every one was occupied.

Moira shouted to be heard over the din. "We'll have to stand for a bit." She was already swaying her hips to the music. The band—a drummer, saxophone player, pianist, and a short man on a double bass that was bigger than he was—struck up an instrumental version of "I Wish I Could Shimmy Like My Sister Kate." I felt a touch at my elbow and turned to see a nice-looking man about my age mouth the word *dance?* I nodded, and followed him onto the dark wooden dance floor. I saw that his friend had taken Moira's hand and was leading her to the same place. A few couples were doing the Charleston, but my partner led me in a lively foxtrot.

The tension of the past days, weeks, months, years fell away, swirled up and swept clean by the music and pure joy of dancing. When the song ended, we joined the men at their table. We'd barely sat down when Moira grabbed my arm and pulled me toward her to speak in my ear.

"Isn't that the gorgeous man who offered us a ride the first time you came here?"

I followed her gaze to the man standing at the bar. I must have smiled or something because Moira said, "What?" I didn't answer, but excused myself and angled through the gyrating dancers to reach the bar.

"Is this your usual haunt?" I asked when I came beside him.

"Not usual, but I've come a few times," Pax said. "And you? I've seen you here twice now."

"This is my second time. Are you following me?"

He laughed. "I know where you live, Cassie. Why would I need to follow you to a dance club?"

My cheeks flamed. How stupid of me to think we were friends and I could make a joke with him.

"No reason. Sorry." I started to turn when Pax took hold of my hand.

"Shall we dance?" he said.

A guitarist and violinist had joined the band and were playing "The Sheik of Araby." Pax led me onto the dance floor. He was as smooth a dancer as anyone on the professional stage. I relaxed into his arms and let him lead me. The dance floor smelled of cigarettes and sweat. Pax's scent was fresh, like the sea. I breathed it in like lifesaving air.

He leaned his mouth close to my ear. "How's the spell casting coming?"

"Ach," I said. "I'm sure I have them right and yet I don't trust that I do. Does that make sense?"

"Oh, yes. Because you failed once when you thought you were ready, you fear you will fail again. That you will never be ready."

I nodded as he twirled me, then said, "Each day is another one that the sea goblin has Jimmy. I can't stand it."

I felt a soft knock on my shoulder and turned to see Moira dancing by with the same man as before. She raised her eyebrows at me in a clear question. I shrugged as best as I could, and watched her sashay away.

When the song ended, Pax said, "Would you like me to come by in the morning? I could help you study."

Yes, please, I thought. And then: *No. Bad idea.* I was growing a bit too fond of Pax—beyond that he was a good companion. I couldn't let emotions get in the way of saving Jimmy.

But Pax was useful there. He knew things. And I could use someone to practice with. Diana didn't think Pax was suitable, but I didn't see the harm. Every spell could be undone.

"Could we make it the day after?" I said. "Tomorrow is already spoken for."

Pax dipped his head and smiled. By the time I returned to the table and looked back, he was gone.

In the car driving home, Moira said, "Come on. Spill. Do you know him?"

"We met on the beach," I said, keeping my voice casual. "He's teaching at USC and staying at a hotel near me. We run into each other from time to time."

"God," Moira said. "He's dreamy. A professor, you say? Almost makes me wish I'd gone to college instead of taking the job in my father's office."

I'd wanted to go to college once, but the school of magic had superseded that dream. I turned my head and stared out the window, thinking how comfortable and right it had felt in Paxton's arms.

~

*E*arly the next morning, my phone rang.

"Mother," I said as I picked up.

"How did you know it was me?" she asked.

"Easy enough to guess." I didn't have to say why—it was Jimmy's fifth birthday.

"Are you engaged today?" she asked.

"No," I said. "Completely free." Because I'd told Diana I had something I had to do today—in case Mother needed company.

A deep sigh came across the line.

"I can't bear to be in the house today," Mother said. "The house where he was born."

"I know," I said.

Her voice brightened. "How about a hike in Griffith Park?"

"I'd like that," I said. "I'll be there in an hour or so."

The park was as wild as Colonel Griffith himself had been, going from man-about-town to San Quentin prisoner after he shot his wife. Father had done business with Griffith, some sort of real estate exchange. I'd met him once when he came to the house, but hadn't liked him. He was too puffed up with himself for my taste.

I did like his park, though, the untamed nature of it. That love of the untamed was probably the main reason I preferred to live by the ocean. Mother had packed a lunch, and after we'd walked enough to feel hungry we settled at one of the park's picnic areas and had our meal. We seemed to have an unspoken agreement not to mention Jimmy's name or what day this was, but I was sure he was in her thoughts, every bit or more as he was in mine.

We went back to the big house and I had dinner with Mother, and then went home—to the beach.

~

*I*n the morning I found myself humming while I dressed, and stopped the moment I realized it. I couldn't remember the last time I'd felt happy enough to hum. Probably only a day here and there since Father went away to war, and that had been years ago. I'd worried every day while he was gone. Then he came home and caught influenza, likely from one of his patients, which brought the gremhahn to us. I supposed I was happy during the years between Father's cure and Jimmy's disappearance. I was happy today because I felt close to breaking the curses and saving my brother. And, I had to admit, a little because Pax was coming.

I finished dressing and put on the kettle. The steam was just starting to cause a whistle when Scout jumped up and trotted toward the front door. A moment later, there was a knock.

Pax had dressed casually in white cotton gabardine trousers, a light blue shirt, and a dark blue suit jacket pinstriped with white. I wore trousers as well, wanting to be comfortable during any spell-casting we might do today.

Scout wriggled out of the front door and jumped up, her paws pressed to his legs, her tail wagging.

"Looks like she's ready for a walk," he said. "The ocean is fine today."

Scout did need a walk. I had all day to work on the spells, so why leave the poor dog antsy and full of energy? I grabbed her leash and the three of us made our way through the families with children, couples, groups of friends, an older man and woman collecting shells, down to the water line, far out now at low tide. The ocean was living up to the name Pacific, as calm as a lake with only the smallest of waves rolling in. I breathed in the fresh scents of salt and sand.

"You said last night that you felt sure and unsure about the spells," Pax said. "Do you want to try one out now?"

I blinked, taken aback. "There are an awful lot of people around. Don't you think it would be better to wait until we're more alone?"

Even though the day was cool to chilly, Hermosa's year-round population was growing and the tourist numbers exploding. It was getting harder and harder to have the beach to myself.

"You don't have a spell to hide what you're doing from others?" he asked.

Of course I did. It was one of the first spells I'd asked for and learned, yet I'd never tried it in public. I knew it worked, though. I'd hidden myself from Scout when moments earlier I'd stood right in front of her, and had watched her dash madly around the house looking for me.

"I have a cloaking spell. Essentially, it will make us invisible to anyone looking our way. Their eyes will fill in background where we are, so in effect they don't see us."

Pax glanced around at the people near us. "Try it."

I steeled myself, recited the words low and made the hand motions that went with them. The words did have to be said out loud—you couldn't just "think" a spell and have it work—but you didn't have to be noisy about it.

When I'd finished, Pax said, "Look. There are seals in the surf."

I was sure no seals had been in the water only moments before. When had they swum in?

The people near us did seem to be looking through and past us, their focus also on the seals. I was a bit thrilled with myself that it worked on humans as well as dogs.

"Call a seal to you," he said.

I'd practiced the summoning spell so many times I didn't have to think twice to recite it. I picked out a seal in the—herd? pack? whatever they were—a light tan pup with big brown eyes, and cast the spell. The seal waded out of the water and made its way up the sand. Beachgoers pointed at the pup and a few moved toward it.

That was no good. The pup was under my spell. It would come to me as directly as if I pulled it on a string. People would follow it and soon enough bump into something they couldn't see, or leave Pax, Scout, and me madly dodging the curious throng. I quickly cast the cloaking spell over the seal, and then a quick spell of forgetfulness for the people who'd seen the pup come out of the water.

I blew out a hard breath. Diana had more than once said, "Think through the possible consequences before you cast the spell." I could see why.

Pax seemed to notice only that I'd bespelled the seal to come out of the water. He laughed and ran down to meet the animal. Scout and I followed behind.

He squatted over his ankles and chucked the seal under the chin, the same way he had Scout—winning her dog heart forever. Scout, for her part, didn't seem too sure about the seal at all. She kept a wary distance, taking one step toward the strange animal, then two steps back, or dancing sideways.

A thought struck me. "Is it you the seal is reacting to," I said to Pax, "or is it an effect of the spell? Does magic also make the enchanted more cooperative?"

He looked up. "The pup is reacting to me, I think. I have a way with dogs and seals. They seem to know I mean them no harm. Come say hello."

I knelt in the sand and tentatively reached toward the seal. It didn't shy away. Its fur was wet and salty but soft. It made little grunting noises when I rubbed its cheeks.

The seals in the water were getting noisy, barking and swimming in what looked to me like an agitated manner—worried about the little pup, I thought.

"I think it should go back now," I said.

Pax nodded and pulled to his feet. I said the release spell and the now again visible pup waddled back into the ocean. When the pup reached the seal group, they dove almost as one and disappeared.

"You did well," Pax said.

"Not as well as I should have."

I told him about the mistakes I'd made in not cloaking the seal the moment it left the water. How I'd had to cast two more spells in a hurry to fix my error. How I'd worried about someone falling over an invisible seal or dog.

"That's what dry runs are for," he said. "To work out the kinks. You saw there were problems and quickly fixed them. Kudos to you."

I smiled without humor. "I suppose so."

"Now, why don't you try the binding spell on me," he said as we walked down the tideline. "And then the release spell."

A jolt of nerves shot through me. I'd practiced the binding

spell until I was blue in the face, and yet still didn't feel confident casting it again on a human. Not after Mother.

Pax gently touched my shoulder. "It'll be all right. Trust yourself."

I nodded but still worried about having him as my test subject.

He waited. I cast the spell.

If I did it right, the binding spell would compel the bound to tell only the truth. The surest way to know if I'd done it right was to make him say something he wouldn't want known.

I swallowed hard and said, "Tell me your deepest secret, the one thing you don't want me to know."

My stomach felt queasy. It was a horrible thing to ask of anyone, but I had to know if the spell worked.

Pax tilted his head as if running through his secrets, deciding which one he most didn't want to reveal.

"The sea is my home," he said.

I didn't know why that was such a deep secret. Probably, he was a sailor. You live at the beach long enough, you know plenty of people who consider the sea their home. I muttered the release spell.

Pax blinked. "You look disappointed."

"It didn't work," I said. "I'm not ready."

Pax laughed lightly. "Oh, it worked all right. I can tell you that."

"How?"

He considered. "A feeling came over me, a desperate need to do whatever you requested, answer any question you asked, do whatever you commanded, be whatever you wanted. It was a very odd feeling. I didn't care for it."

"But you're sure the spell worked?"

"Absolutely. And obviously the release spell works, too. If

you've mastered all your enchantments as well as those two, I'd say you're ready."

I might be ready, but the first spell that needed to be cast after I'd summoned the sea goblin needed three, and Mother clearly wasn't up to it.

FIFTEEN

Hermosa Beach, California
July 1924

*T*he darkness of deep night was no different whether my eyes were closed or open. I lay awake in my bed, my thoughts chasing around and around.

Was I ready to take on the sea goblin?

I knew every spell I needed backwards and forwards.

Except, every time I'd thought this before, I'd been wrong. But I'd learned from each misstep. I was ready now.

Only, Diana had said I needed to find my ally before I attempted to get Jimmy back. Had I found the one?

I was pretty sure I had. And why couldn't my ally be the third voice needed to break the curses on Mother and me? Diana never said Mother had to be the third voice.

I got out of bed. Scout woke and padded beside me down the stairs and to the kitchen. I pressed the button for the electric lights Father had had installed a few years back and found the paper with the number I wanted. It was late. Too late to be phoning, but I did anyway.

The night manager snorted when I asked for him to please wake his guest and ask him to come to the phone, but the manager did it.

"Cassie?" Pax said, his voice both sleepy and worried.

"I know it's late. I apologize for waking you. Would you come to my house tomorrow? I have a large favor to ask and would like to do it face to face."

Silence answered my question, but then Pax said, "Of course. I can come now, if you like."

≈

*P*ax looked remarkably awake and fresh for a man dragged from his warm, comfortable bed in the middle of the night so I could ask him to be the third curse-breaker. Now, I wasn't sure that was a good idea after all. What if it had to be all women? What if it had to be both Mother and me—the cursed ones? I should have thought this through and spoken with Diana first.

Pax followed me into the parlor and sat on the sofa. Scout immediately settled herself across his feet and closed her eyes contentedly.

"Can I get you anything?" I said. "Water? Tea?"

"No," he said. "Thank you."

I sat in the chair opposite the sofa and clasped my hands in my lap.

Pax watched me, curiosity clear in his eyes. "Just ask, Cassie."

A nervous tingle skittered through my stomach. Just ask. Easier said than done. I screwed up my courage and said, "I wondered if you'd be willing to help me break the curses the gremhahn laid on Mother and myself."

Pax regarded me evenly. "What sort of curses?"

I told him the tale, how Mother and I had caught the sea

goblin, how Mother had beaten him with the steel bar, how he'd thrown the shell into the sea, the details of the curse on Mother and the one on me, and how it took three to break the curses.

"That's quite a story," he said when I'd finished.

My heart sank. He'd seen magic firsthand—felt the effect of the binding spell—and he thought this was a fiction?

"You don't believe me," I said, and crossed to sit next to him on the sofa. "I can prove it's true." I turned the back of my head toward him and pulled out the pins that held my hair in a bun, letting it fall free.

"Look closely. There are tiny stars in my hair. Eleven of them. One for every month since the gremhahn laid his curse on me."

His fingers moved gently but skillfully through my hair. A shiver ran through me at his touch, followed by a feeling of *rightness*, as if I'd waited all my life for this one thing and now it was here. I wanted his hands on me, to feel his warmth, his strength. I wanted to turn and feel his lips on mine.

Pax drew in a sharp breath. "Oh, Cassie," he said so softly I could barely hear him. "This must be horrible for you."

I pulled away sharply and swiveled to face him.

"Inconvenient," I said.

The gremhahn would be amused to see me know—the proof of his curse being the very thing that made me crave the one event the curse forbade: intimacy with a man.

"I have to keep my hair pinned up," I said, tossing the words off lightly, "and of course I can't go to the beauty parlor. It's fortunate my hairstyle doesn't need much upkeep."

Pax chuckled under his breath, then sobered.

"I believe you, Cassie—about everything. And I sorely wish I could help."

My heart sank further. "But you won't."

"Not won't," he said. "Can't, for reasons that need to stay private."

I bit my bottom lip, considering his words. Everyone had secrets. I'd not ask Pax to give up any more of his.

"It's a lovely night," he said, obviously changing the subject. "Shall we walk by the water?"

"It's two in the morning," I said.

"We'll have the beach all to ourselves." He rose carefully to his feet so as not to startle Scout. She pulled herself up and stretched, then looked from me to Pax and wagged her tail. *Walk* was a word she knew well.

"Let me get her leash," I said.

A thick cloud layer covered the sky. The moon and stars were hazy, like seeing them through waxed paper. The air smelled strongly of sulfur from the earlier Independence Day fireworks, which I'd watched from my porch. Confetti streamers and dead sparklers littered the sand. The tide was out and the waves rolled gently onto the shore, their sound a lullaby. I unhooked Scout's leash, but this late at night there was little to chase and she mostly snuffled the sand near us.

A seagull cried and I looked up, surprised. I hadn't thought gulls flew at night. It circled us once, then dropped something it held in its beak—a small white shell.

Pax bent to retrieve it. Not a *Murex ramosus*, but an ordinary clam shell, a kind that was common here.

"From the gremhahn," I said, half-question, half-statement of fact.

"I'd say so," Pax said.

"Why?"

He thought about it. "To let you know he's watching."

Fear shot through me. If the goblin was keeping an eye on me, he could know about the magic I was learning, that it was all to break the curses and get my brother back. It gave him time to prepare a defense—or a counter-offense.

"Then he knows everything," I said.

"Maybe not," Pax said. "If he's dependent on what he or his servants actually saw or heard, he may know much less than everything. He may know only what happens near the water."

"But I can't be sure."

"No," he said, "you can't. You may want to do all your practices indoors from now on."

I thought about the spells I'd cast in Diana's backyard and in my own. Seagulls flew over often enough that it wasn't something I'd ordinarily notice. Now I wondered if any of those birds were the goblin's spies or the gremhahn himself. How much did he know of our plans? Surely the sea goblin knew of my little trick with the seal. That alone would tell him that I had magic about me.

Pax gently squeezed my shoulder, offering sympathy, I thought.

Lightning seemed to zing through me at his touch. I wanted to sink into him.

I shrugged my shoulder free of his hand and moved a step away.

I'd been less than completely truthful when I'd told Pax about the curse on me, saying only that I could never have children. I'd skipped right over the reason why love and marriage weren't for me. No man would be pleased to see his lover turn to dust in his bed.

"I'm sorry," I said. "I need to think."

"My hand on your shoulder stops your brain?" Pax said softly.

I could still feel the warmth of his touch. "You're distracting."

Pax smiled. "That's good."

No, it wasn't good. Not at all good.

He took a step toward me, closing the gap between us. "I like you too, Cassie."

"This is not the time or place," I said, my voice quavering the slightest bit.

"It's exactly the time and place," he said.

Was Pax part of the gremhahn's cruelty—a handsome demon sent to tempt and destroy me?

I knew I should run, but his scent and the warmth of his body drew me like the promise of water to the parched.

He put both arms around me and kissed my mouth. A deep kiss. A kiss the likes of which no one had ever given me before. I broke away from him, breathless. I thought turning to dust might be worth it.

The starfish at my throat grew warm. The warmth spread over my skin and into my core. I felt stronger, more aware, more focused than I could remember ever feeling. And confident. So what if the gremhahn had been keeping an eye on me. I knew my spells. I was a competent and able mage. I'd break the curses. I'd get Jimmy back. And then, maybe—

But until then . . .

Pax walked Scout and me back to my house but said goodbye on the porch. I didn't know if he would kiss me again, if I should kiss him. Did I want to kiss him again? I stood with my hand on the doorknob, hesitating, unable to decide on the answer.

He decided for me—planting a quick kiss on the top of my head and then leaving without a word. A lovely thrill spread through me, starting from the crown of my head and melting its way to my toes.

I went inside, closed the door behind me and leaned against it a moment.

"Paxton Yeager," I whispered. "Pax."

Jimmy, I thought. And Mother.

≈

*T*hree a.m. Four a.m. Four thirty. I gave up trying to sleep and slid from my bed. Scout raised her head from where she'd been sleeping at the end of the bed. I put a finger to my lips.

"Shhh. Go back to sleep. I'm going for a walk."

Her ears twitched at the word *walk*, but evidently sleep was a more appealing idea. She lay her head back down and closed her eyes. I dressed in trousers and a light sweater and padded barefoot onto the sand and down to the sea.

The clouds that had blurred the stars had drifted away, leaving a canopy of lights overhead. I stared out over the dark water and fingered one of the stars in my hair, its cold hardness and all it represented spurring my growing fury. The goblin had cursed Mother never to see her son again. He'd cursed me never to marry or know passion with a man. Neither Mother nor I would ever be free to live our lives fully until the curses were broken and Jimmy returned to his human form. My brother's year as a seal was drawing close to its final days.

I paced along the waterline, anger making my steps hard and fast. I'd bring the gremhahn to his knees, leave him begging to free us all from his curses. I'd make him sorry for the day he'd first knocked on our door and for stealing my brother.

Under my breath, I muttered the calling spell, not realizing it until the last word had left my lips. I clamped my mouth shut and stood dead still. I hoped beyond hope the spell hadn't worked, though I knew I'd memorized it and practiced until pronouncing every word perfectly was second nature.

A waterspout rose suddenly in front of me, huge and dark, rising toward the sky. Drops of water and flecks of foam sprayed onto my face and body. As quickly as it had come, the spout sucked back into the ocean, forming a vortex that pulled the water around it down and around. The shore water sucked at my feet and ankles, trying to pull me in. I braced one foot in front of the other to stop from falling.

And then the goblin was in the shallows, standing right in front of me. He wore the body and face of Dr. Gremhahn. His eyes were narrowed, his nostrils flared, his mouth curled into a sneer. The dark wool-like suit he wore was dry as desert sand as he rose from the water.

"Oh, it's you," he said, his voice full of contempt.

I started the personal protection spell, saying the words fast so the sea goblin would have little chance to stop me.

He leapt forward, knocking me to the sand, and cutting off my words. He fell on top of me, sitting on my chest, his legs straddling my body. I tried to shake him off as I started the protection spell again. He grabbed a handful of wet sand and shoved it into my mouth. I swung my head from side to side and tried to spit out the sandy mud, but he kept his hand over my mouth no matter how hard I tried to dislodge it.

"Spit out your nasty spells now," he said, contempt darkening his words. "Stupid girl. You and your stupid mother, thinking you could best me with your infantile magic."

I swung my shoulders again to knock the goblin off. He laughed and pressed his hand harder against my mouth. I gagged on the wet sand.

The starfish at my throat warmed, growing hot, sending strength and energy deep into me. I screamed through the mud and his hand, out into the darkened night. The scream surprised him, and in that brief moment of hesitation he lessened the pressure on my mouth and his weight on my body. I focused on twisting my chest and shoulders to the side and up at the same moment. The gremhahn lost his hold and balance and tumbled off me into the sand.

I jumped to my feet and started the protection spell again. The goblin rolled over onto his hands and knees, then jumped up to his feet. He was laughing, his fingers poked into his ears. The waves rose offshore, growing higher and higher, crashing against the beach, drowning out my words. If he couldn't hear me, the spell wouldn't work. I could call him from a distance, but he had to hear my words for me to be safe. I shouted into the cacophony of the waves but I couldn't even hear myself.

The gremhahn began to grow—just as he had when he'd become a fish that day with Mother. But his height didn't frighten me now. I had a weapon against that.

I pronounced the levitation spell and began rising into the air, keeping my face even with his but backing off as he grew, to stay out of his reach.

"However big you can grow," I shouted over the waves, "I can go higher. You will never rise above me, even if your head pokes through the clouds."

It was a bold lie, and he likely couldn't hear me anyway, but his growing stopped. I started the protection spell a third time. The gremhahn laughed, snapped his fingers, and was gone.

No, not gone. Turned into a crab the size of my palm, scuttling toward the water.

Clever of him, I thought as I descended back to the sand. Crabs don't have ears. But there had to be a way to make him hear the spell. There had to be.

The crab was nearly at the water. If he made it in, I'd lose him. I could use the calling spell again, but if he stayed a crab — I ran toward the water and snatched up the gremhahn with two hands just before he made it to safety. He sank both pincers into my skin. I cried out but didn't turn him loose. He tightened his hold. I gritted my teeth and began the protection spell a fourth time, hoping I could get it all said before the gremhahn stopped me again. Crabs may not have ears, but the sea goblin did, and it was the sea goblin I held in my hand, no matter what he looked like.

The pincers slowly loosened when I finished the spell. I held the crab between my hands and breathed hard, letting my skin forget the pain of the pinches. The crab wasn't moving. Slowly I drew my two hands apart. A sob rose in my throat. All I held was an empty shell. I threw it down in disgust.

A gust of wind blew over my head, and I looked up. The biggest bird I'd ever seen was diving at me. *Albatross*, my stunned mind managed to whisper. The sound of its wings was like a storm. Its body was as big as Molly's had been. The bird was nearly twice my height, wing to wing, and flying right at me. Hatred glared in its dark, glittering eyes. I wanted to run, but my feet wouldn't move. Something that big and heavy hitting me would cause damage, maybe permanently.

I remembered my vision at Diana's—a seagull. But maybe that was because I thought of those birds in connection with the sea goblin. I hadn't seen him hide as an albatross before. But I was still the arrow. There was no time for a personal protection spell now. I started reciting the levitation spell, holding off the last word until the albatross was almost on me, its wings folded, diving down. I screamed the last word and focused all my attention on rising to meet the bird. The bird opened its beak—the curve at the end as sharp as a hook —and screamed back at me. Just as we were about to collide, I shifted aside of its path. It couldn't stop or turn as fast as I could. As it flew past, I grabbed its neck.

The thing let out a strangled cry and flew toward the sky. I hung on, desperately trying to figure out how to make the bird turn and go back to the ground. I couldn't let go. Maybe the levitation spell would stop me from falling, but maybe not. A fall from this height could kill me.

The beach receded below. I held tight with both hands to the bird's neck and watched as it turned toward the sea. My heart pounded in my chest. If I didn't let go soon, the bird could take me so far out across the ocean that even if I could land gently on the water, I'd never be able to swim to shore.

I focused hard and made myself let one hand come free. I doubled that hand into a fist and punched the bird's breast as hard as I could, aiming for the heart. My fist thudded into the bird's body. Bone cracked beneath my blow. We tumbled toward the water.

I spit out the levitation spell as fast as I could make my lips and tongue move. My body jerked as my fall slowed but didn't stop. The goblin dropped into the sea with a huge splash and disappeared. The sea was his home—he'd be fine. Probably turn into a fish and swim away.

He had to be fine. I needed him to get Jimmy back.

I hit the water. Not hard enough to break something, but still it hurt. Cold ocean water shocked my senses to full alert. I grabbed a last, desperate gulp of air as the water closed over my head, momentum from the fall carrying me down and down. All I saw was water as I plunged deeper into the sea. My lungs began to ache.

Something bumped me from below. Something big.

Shark, I thought, terrified so deeply I almost let go of what little oxygen I was still holding in my lungs. I flailed my arms, hoping to scare it off and to stop my downward fall.

Whatever was below bumped me again. I turned my head and caught sight of not the shark I'd feared, but a large harbor seal. It nudged me again, pushing me upwards. Water rushed over me, parting as we raced toward the surface. The seal shoved me up through the last of the water and into the air, then dove, disappearing in the dark sea. I treaded water and gulped fresh oxygen into my lungs.

The seal, its white spots gleaming in the moonlight, surfaced again next to me and bobbed alongside while I caught my breath. I reached a hand toward it, but it dove and disappeared. Whatever help it had to offer seemed finished now.

A cold breeze blew against my skin. The smell of salt stung my nose. A clump of brown seaweed floated nearby, rising and falling on the tide. I treaded water, moving in a slow circle, trying to figure out where I was.

It was hard to see anything in the moonlight. I couldn't see the beach, but the swells seemed to be moving in one direction, which I figured had to be toward shore. But if I couldn't see land I was likely too far out to swim to safety before exhaustion overwhelmed me. And maybe the swells didn't go to the shore at all.

I couldn't stay where I was. It would be too easy for the sea goblin to find me and pull me under. *Pick a direction and go*, I told myself.

A splash sounded behind me. I spun, terrified it was the gremhahn.

The spotted seal rolled onto its side and extended a flipper toward me. I'd never heard of a seal attacking a person, but anything was possible—especially if this wasn't really a seal, but the sea goblin himself. He could look like anyone, anything. How could I know what to trust?

The seal slapped its flipper on the water, splashing water into my face, then held its flipper out to me again. I reached out and gently touched the limb. The seal wriggled toward me, shoving its flipper into my open hand. I held on as best I could. The seal seemed happy with that, but then pulled its flipper away and swam under me, coming up so that I sat on its back. I leaned forward and wrapped my arms around its neck. Its fur was wet but sleek and soft. The seal's warmth radiated into my shivering body. I figured that if this were the sea goblin in disguise and he dove underwater, I could always let go.

The seal stayed on top of the water, though, cutting through it like a blade. I lifted my head as high as I could while keeping my arms around the seal's neck, and watched for shore. I hoped it was shore we were heading to.

Another seal rose near us—not so large as the one I rode, but big and sturdy enough. In its mouth, it was holding Dr. Gremhahn by the arm. Which meant the seal I was riding wasn't the sea goblin. That was a relief, at least. The seal holding the goblin dove under the water. I thought I saw its wake trailing behind us.

After a time, the swells grew larger and rougher, and I could make out the dim outline of the beach. I held onto the seal as we came close to where the waves were breaking. The seal stopped and seemed to be thinking for a moment, then caught a rising swell. Together we rode the wave in to shore, landing on the sand with a thud. I hauled in a breath, scarcely able to believe what had happened, and rolled off the seal onto the wet sand.

"Thank you," I said. "I've heard of dolphins bringing sailors to land, but never a seal." I levered myself to my knees and kissed the animal's nose.

The second seal waded onto the shore, dragging the sea goblin with it. The goblin hit the side of the seal's head with his free arm. I guessed the seal didn't like that, since it shook the gremhahn like an errant piece of seaweed, then threw him hard onto the sand near me, knocking the goblin senseless.

The seal that had saved me barked, then made its way back to the water and disappeared under the waves. The second seal followed closely behind.

The sea goblin had been knocked out by the throw, but was coming around. I shouted out the protection spell and then the binding spell before he could regain his wits and do anything to stop me. By the way his face screwed up, I knew the spell had worked. A smile spread across my lips. He was bound to me now and had to tell the truth.

"Where's my brother?" I said. "Where's Jimmy?"

"In the sea, where he belongs," the goblin said, pulling himself slowly to his feet.

I didn't like that answer. It could mean too many things. "Is he alive?"

"Oh, yes," the goblin said. "Quite alive. Quite fond of fish." He laughed.

I wanted to hit him for that laugh.

"Return Jimmy to me, now."

The gremhahn shook his head. "I can't do that. He's quite on his own."

I grabbed his shoulders and shook him. "Enough of your double-talk. Give me back my brother, right this moment."

The sea goblin slowly turned his head to look out to the water. "I have no control over your brother. Maybe you could do one of your little spells on him, eh? That might work."

I didn't trust the goblin; there was probably a trick in there somewhere, but he was still under my command and had to tell the truth. I turned his shoulders loose and cast the calling spell to Jimmy. All that came was a small group of seals, bobbing in the surf. My heart sank. One young pup swam forward, coming almost to the shore.

"There's your brother," the goblin said. "Take him home, why don't you?"

I grabbed him by the shoulders again. "Change Jimmy back."

"Do you have a spell for that, Mage?" the goblin said. "You

have bound me to speak the truth. The truth is I can change a boy into a seal, but cannot change a seal into a boy. So if you have a spell to do that, pronounce it now. If not, best set me free. Or perhaps you will take me home, keep your brother and me as pets. You still live in that nice beach cottage?"

I wanted to slap him. I wanted to throw him in the water and push his head into the sand until he suffocated. Tears stung my eyes. So close, and yet not close at all.

The seal that was Jimmy had waded onto the shore but seemed afraid to come any closer.

"I'll be back, Jimmy," I called. "I'll be back and everything will be fine. I promise."

SIXTEEN

Hermosa Beach, California
July 1924

I'd hardly slept after my meeting with the gremhahn but couldn't settle down from the angry energy pulsing through me. I paced through the house, Scout worrying at my heels. What sort of idiot was I to mutter a spell without even knowing it? Worse, to call the gremhahn without realizing it, without a plan, leaving myself at the disadvantage. Diana was right—I wasn't ready.

"I'm completely useless," I said to Scout. She sat, thumped her tail a couple of times, and looked up at me, her brown eyes soulful. For the first time I could remember, she failed to melt my heart or lift my foul mood.

I headed out the door to a sun-filled morning. I had nowhere I needed to be, no place I was heading. I loved the beach and the ocean—and wanted nothing to do with either today. I left Scout behind as well, lacking the patience to wait for a curious dog that wanted to stop and sniff each new smell on the street. I wanted to walk, to stomp, to burn off the frustration roiling through me and shut down the mind that wouldn't stop saying Jimmy had only days left in which to be rescued and what a cretin I was.

Passing Kerwin's Bakery I saw Pax sitting inside, alone at a window table. I didn't want to talk to him. I had no interest in reliving the experience with the gremhahn while telling the tale. On the other hand, I couldn't imagine making small talk while all I could think about was what had happened. I quickly crossed the street, then marched up Santa Fe to Hermosa Avenue and turned right.

I strode down the asphalt road, frustration driving my feet past homes, businesses, and empty lots on the street. Sand dunes dotted with wild barley and yellow pincushion flowers rose to the east as I walked out of Hermosa and into Redondo Beach, stopping only when thirst drove me into a small market. I took a Coca-Cola from the cooler, snapped off the lid on the bottle opener on the cooler's side, and recovered my manners enough to politely pay a nickel to the thin woman in a floral dress behind the counter. Outside, I leaned against the market's green stucco wall and took a deep drink of the cold soda pop.

Stop acting like a baby, I told myself. *All this berating yourself isn't accomplishing a thing.*

I took another swallow of soda, surprised that the next thought that came to me was *Talk to Pax.*

I needed to tell someone what had happened, that much at least had come clear to me now, lest it chase around and around in my mind forever. Pax was a good choice, I thought. He seemed a steady-hand-on-the-tiller sort, something in between Diana's cool, clinical eye and Mother's natural tendency to support me no matter what. I finished the Coke, returned the bottle to the thin woman, and headed to Hermosa.

Of course, Pax had left Kerwin's by the time I arrived. I went to the Berth Hotel, but Jack Masters, who was working the desk, looked over his shoulder and said, "The room key is here. He must be out."

Disappointed, but at least no longer full of fury, I headed home. Scout needed a walk—a nice calm one. It'd be good for both of us.

Pax was sitting in one of the white wicker chairs on the porch when I got there. He rose when he saw me coming and doffed his straw boater.

"What are you doing here?" I said in a surprised-to-see-you voice.

He held his hat loosely at one side. "I spotted you this morning hiking up Santa Fe Avenue as if the street was on fire a block behind you," he said. "I thought you might like some company."

"Thank you," I said, fishing in my handbag for the house key. "I could. Yes."

I found the key and opened the front door. Scout was waiting in the foyer, her tail wagging. I knelt down, rubbed her chest, and said hello, sorry now that I'd virtually ignored her in my stew this morning.

"I'll put the kettle on," I said as I stood, and directed Pax with my eyes into the parlor. Scout followed me to the kitchen. I scratched behind her ears and gave her a biscuit while waiting for the water to boil.

I brought two cups of strong, sweet tea and a plate of sugar cookies and set them on the end table next to the sofa. I handed Pax his cup, took my own and sat in the chair facing him. Pax held his cup in his lap and looked at me.

"Something happened after I left last night," he said, making it a firm statement, no question in his voice.

I lowered my cup and sighed. "I couldn't sleep. I went down to the water."

Pax set his cup on the side table and leaned toward me, listening.

"I went down to the water," I began again. "I was thinking ahead to the day when I'd call the gremhahn, break the spells and get my brother back and—" I cleared my throat. "I didn't realize I was doing it, but I spoke the calling spell out loud."

He took that in. "And what happened?"

I laughed ruefully. "The spell worked. I guess I should be glad for knowing that."

He had his eyes fixed on my mouth, seeing as well as hearing my words—as if he wanted to be extra sure he got them correct.

"Jimmy isn't in a shell," I said. "The gremhahn had turned him into a seal, the same as you'd told me. I guess the folktales are true."

"They often are," Pax said.

I folded my arms over my chest, as if that would keep anger and grief from tearing me apart. "I couldn't make the gremhahn turn him back." Tears sprung to my eyes. "My brother was right there in front of me and I had to leave him on the beach because I'd assumed the binding spell could make the sea goblin turn my brother back into a boy."

Pax nodded, but said, "Why didn't it work?"

"The goblin said that once Jimmy was changed, he couldn't change him back. I guess his was a one-way spell."

"There's a Scottish tale like that," he said, his voice soft and calming. "A peasant, out poaching one day, stumbles into the part of the forest where an ogre is chained to a tree. The peasant says if the ogre will change the peasant's pocketfuls of dirt into pocketfuls of gold, the peasant will free the ogre. The ogre does, but the peasant runs off, leaving the ogre chained up. The ogre can't do anything about it because changing the dirt was one-way magic. The moral of the story is that no one can think of everything."

His words eased my guilt, but they didn't solve the problem.

"There has to be a way to change Jimmy back, or there's no point to any of this," I said. "If the stories say the stolen children can be returned to their families so long as a year hasn't passed, there must be a way to restore them. How is that done?"

Pax took a sip of tea before he answered. "I don't know. The stories gloss over that part, saying something along the lines of 'And the child was returned to its natural state' without explaining how it happened."

I stared at him. Was he trying to tell me it was hopeless, that I should give up? If he thought I would, he didn't know me at all.

"I have magic, Pax. I'll make the sea goblin return my brother."

He hiked one shoulder in a half-shrug of agreement. "Perhaps you should go see Diana. Tell her what happened. She'll help if she can."

I nodded, glumly. I didn't much fancy telling her what a fool I'd been, but I'd have to take my lumps about it.

"I'm sorry, but I should be going," he said, setting down his cup and saucer and coming to his feet. "I have an appointment with an old friend."

"Oh," I said, disappointed. If there was ever a time I needed company, this was it. I hadn't told him yet about the gremhahn becoming an albatross or how I'd fallen into the sea and was rescued by a seal.

Scout nosed the back of my knee. I reached back and stroked her head, wondering what other tricks the sea goblin had that I needed to prepare for. As Pax had said, no one can think of everything.

"Cassie," he said. "Whatever happens, in the end you will prevail. Trust yourself."

I smiled weakly. "Thank you."

At the door, he kissed me lightly on the corner of my mouth and said, "Talk to Diana."

~

*D*iana's red door seemed more forbidding than friendly as I stood on the porch, hesitant. The door swung open just as I was steeling myself to knock, and I saw the surprised look on Diana's face. She hid it well. It lasted only an instant as she said goodbye to a woman not much older than myself, wearing a blue-and-white-striped visiting dress. I assumed she was a client from the brief conversation between them.

"Come in," Diana said when the woman had reached the street. "You look like you have something to say."

I didn't know if it was good or bad that I was so transparent.

I sat on the sofa in the parlor and told Diana all that had happened with the gremhahn. I saw frustration in her narrowed eyes and in the tightening of her mouth while I spoke. When I finished, she was silent.

"Honestly, Cassie," she said finally. "If you saving your brother wasn't ordained, I wouldn't teach you another thing. When this is over, I may put a spell of forgetfulness on you and wipe out all your magical knowledge. I don't think you can be trusted with it."

I held my head high. I'd done nothing to be ashamed of—not the way she was thinking of it. "I haven't misused the magic. I've been underprepared, but no one can think of everything. And—I did think of something. A way to save Jimmy without the sea goblin's help."

Her eyebrows shot upward. "Oh?"

I was a little proud of myself for having thought of this on the way over and could hear the excitement in my voice when I spoke.

"I learned this morning that Jimmy isn't under the gremhahn's control. Once the goblin turned Jimmy into a seal, he lost all power over him. So, I can use the calling spell to bring my brother to me. All I need is to learn a spell that will undo the enchantment."

"All you need," Diana said with a scoff. "Unfortunately doing that still takes three, just as it takes three for curse breaking, and your mother—"

I knew the rest of it: Mother wasn't ready and Pax couldn't, or wouldn't, help.

"Why do the spells to take off the curses and to restore Jimmy take three?" I asked, hearing the frustration in my own voice. It seemed I could do everything else necessary by myself, but these two things needed help.

"Because it is much easier to do than to undo," she said.

I scratched at the back of my head, thinking. My fingers caught on a star. I pulled my hand away.

I thought it likely Mother had told Diana about my stars and the curse they represented, but I hadn't told her myself. She never let on if she knew. I swallowed down the anger touching one of those stars always brought on in me. There were other things I needed to focus on now.

"What about your nephew?" I said. "The one I brought with the calling spell. He's studying magic. Could he be the third?"

Diana shook her head. "It has to be you and Audrey."

"Family members only?"

"Not necessarily, but emotionally involved," she said. "That kind of magic—breaking curses and undoing a spell that has passed out of the control of the original caster—

depends much on emotional connections. If you hired three random mages to do the job, they wouldn't be able to change your brother back because they'd have no *heart* in the magic."

"Jimmy only has a few days left," I said.

"I know," she said.

I took one of her hands in both of mine. "You have to ask Mother to do it. If she doesn't feel ready, she'll tell you. It has to be you that asks. If I ask, she'd say yes no matter what."

Diana gently freed her hand. "She'll say yes no matter who asks her. Jimmy is her son."

"Then use magic to make her ready, to make her strong," I said. "If she finds out later that we didn't do everything possible to save Jimmy—"

My voice trailed off. The rest of that sentence was *she'd never forgive herself*.

I think Diana had realized the truth of my unspoken words herself. She was quiet a long moment.

"There is a spell that will give your mother the strength she needs," she said, "but afterwards—"

"Afterwards what?"

"It'll burn up all the magic that's in her."

Worry shot through me. "Burn up?"

Diana shook her head. "She won't feel any pain, but her magic will be completely gone. Completely destroyed."

I bit my bottom lip. "Magic makes her sick anyway. She'll likely be glad to be rid of it."

Diana half nodded. "You might be right. It might even be a favor for her."

"You can ask," I said, but I knew Mother would say yes. Even if giving up magic broke her heart, getting Jimmy back would mend it, and then some. I knew my mother well enough to know which choice she would make.

"Wait here a moment," Diana said, and disappeared toward the back of the house.

I heard her rummaging around in a rear room I'd never been in. She came back carrying a large book bound in old brown leather. There was writing of some sort in gold on the spine in words I couldn't read. Diana had her finger stuck in the book, marking a place. She opened it, read to herself, then nodded.

"On page 386 is a spell you'll need to make sure the gremhahn won't come back and bother you in the future," she said.

I'd worried about that. We could get Jimmy back, but what was to stop the goblin from showing up the next day and taking him again, or stop him from adding more curses on top of the ones already leveled on Mother and me?

"What sort of spell is it?" I asked.

"It's usually used when a man or woman wants to end unwanted attention from the opposite sex—it dissolves the other person's passion. But I think it will also dissolve the sea goblin's obsession with you and Audrey—because clearly he does have some fascination for you two, or he would have been gone from your lives long ago."

The thought sent shivers down my spine.

"I think you're right about the goblin hating Mother and me, probably because Mother trapped and beat him." My voice dropped low. "I think he tried to kill me this morning."

Diana's eyes widened.

"A seal saved me," I said.

"Cassie, back up," she said. "What do you mean the gremhahn tried to kill you?"

I told her the story. Deep creases formed in her forehead as she listened.

"Let me think on the curse problem," she said, handing me the book. "In the meantime, learn the spell by heart."

She patted the book in my hands as if taking leave of a

good friend. "Go home. I'll call you after I've spoken with your mother."

~

*T*wo days went by with no word from Diana. When I phoned Mother, no one answered. I practiced the new spell and tried not to worry. Mother had her own busy life, but even when I telephoned late in the evening, she didn't pick up. That wasn't like her.

On the morning of the third day, Pax came by.

"Did you bring your car?" I said before I'd even completely opened the front door.

He looked momentarily surprised but quickly regained his composure.

"Is there somewhere you'd like to go?"

"I've been calling my mother for two days, but there's no answer. I'm worried something has happened to her. I was going to take the Red Car over but would appreciate it if you'd drive me to her house."

His brow had furrowed while I talked. "Of course," he said.

If people stared at us as we drove by in his blood-red speedster, I didn't notice. All I could think about was Mother lying hurt in the house or yard, or some other misfortune that might have befallen her. Pax tended to drive fast, but now I wished he'd go even faster.

The moment he stopped in front of the house, I jumped free of the car and ran toward the door. I was just opening it when Mother came around from the side of the house. Dressed in a pair of Father's old trousers, one of his shirts, and thick gardening gloves, she carried a flat of purple-and-yellow pansies.

"I've been calling for days," I said. "Where have you been? I've been worried half out of my wits."

Mother laughed quietly to herself and came toward me. "Here and there, Cassie. I'm sorry if you were worried but as you can see, I'm quite well."

This must happen to every child, I suddenly thought—the moment when you realize your parent is a full person in their own right, with their own life. Funny how we fight so hard to be seen as independent and capable ourselves, but don't allot the same consideration to a parent.

Mother set the flat of flowers down. "Now, why have you been trying so desperately to reach me?"

From the corner of my eye, I caught sight of Pax on the sidewalk. He nodded to me, then walked away, giving me time alone with Mother.

"Have you spoken with Diana?" I asked.

Mother removed her gardening gloves. "Why?"

I'd rather hoped that Diana had already told Mother about my mess-up with the gremhahn, and that I wouldn't have to admit it to her myself. I took a breath and heaved it out.

"I accidently called the sea goblin and tried to get Jimmy returned to us, but the goblin has turned Jimmy into a seal and can't change him back. I've figured a way to lift the spell from Jimmy, I think, but I want to also lift the curses the gremhahn put on you and me, and that has to be done first. Diana says it takes three to do that, but you're not strong enough yet. She can push your strength, but it will wipe out all your magic."

Mother squatted and fiddled with the pansies. I waited, letting her think. She stood again. "Of course I'll help. Being rid of magic for good won't grieve me, and even if it did—"

Her voice trailed off, but I knew the rest of it: She'd do it to get Jimmy back.

"Diana and I discussed this, and we hope you agree," she said. "We'd like to confront the gremhahn Thursday."

A thrill of nerves shot up my breastbone. Thursday was two days away.

SEVENTEEN

Hermosa Beach, California
July 10, 1924

10:45 a.m. 10:46. 10:47. Mother and Diana were to meet me at the house at 11:30. I couldn't stand the waiting. I wrote *On the beach* on a half-sheet of paper, told Scout to stay, and pinned the note to the front door.

The day was fine, the sun a hazy yellow marble in a cloudless blue sky. To the north, the beach was already crowded with people near the pier. Not that many people had staked out spots in front of my house, but there were more than I wanted. I cast a dampening spell and watched as people who'd been perfectly happy with their places on the sand began to look around, suddenly uncomfortable, then pack up and leave. The dampening spell would keep any newcomers away as well. I layered a cloaking spell on top, to make me invisible to anyone glancing across this section of beach, and walked down to the water.

The ocean held its usual summer calmness, small waves coming in and exhausting themselves on the shore. Pelicans in a V-formation flew overhead, heading south toward Redondo Beach. Sandpipers ran along the waterline, pecking at the light layer of film that covered the wet sand. Seagulls cried overhead at their brethren on the land.

"Shoo," I said, turning in a circle and waving my arms at the gulls standing near me. I didn't think every gull was the gremhahn's spy, but I disliked them all on principle.

In the midst of my turn I saw Diana coming across the sand toward me. I glanced at my wristwatch. 11:15. She was early. Mother should be here soon. Nerves shot through me. This was the day and soon would be the moment to confront the sea goblin, when we three, working in concert, would break the curses and get Jimmy back.

My heart thumped and my stomach knotted as I ran through the spells in my head again. I was as ready as I could be and still feared I wasn't ready enough. Diana came up on my left side but said nothing. Her gaze was fixed out across the water.

"Have you used the strength spell with Mother?" I asked.

Diana nodded, but didn't look at me. I followed her gaze. The waves were small but hitting harder when they broke then they had a few minutes earlier. A sudden, strong wind picked up. My straw hat blew off and tumbled down the shore. Thick drifts of sand blew into my face. I closed my eyes against the gritty assault.

When I opened them again, the sea goblin, in his Dr. Gremhahn guise, stood only feet away from us. My stomach lurched. His gaze was focused behind Diana and me, and it was ugly. I glanced over my shoulder toward the Strand. Mother was picking her way across the beach toward us, her shoes in her hand. I started the binding spell to put the goblin in thrall to me and under my command.

"Never!" he screamed before I got all the words out. I lost my place and had to start the spell again.

"I told you," the gremhahn yelled, his eyes still locked past us to Mother. "You will never see your son again."

He drew his fists tight in front of his chest, then thrust his arms up and out, his hands flying open, crying that word again—"Never!"

Mother screamed and threw her hands over her eyes.

"Oh dear God. Help me," Mother said, stumbling to where we stood. "I can't see. I'm blind."

Diana threw her arms around her, as if in protection, but it was too late.

Panic and rage burned through me. We were too late. Too late to break Mother's curse. Too late to save Jimmy. The words of the binding spell flew from my mind as if I'd never known them.

The goblin fixed his harsh gaze on me.

"Pathetic," he said.

I was pathetic, never thinking the goblin might still be keeping watch on me. Nothing like making a big point of being here, especially with Diana arriving just as I was shooing away the seagulls. Which one had flown off to give the gremhahn the news? The goblin wasn't stupid. He likely knew that Jimmy's year was coming to a close, and here were Diana and I on the shore. How smart did he have to be to divine that we'd come for him? Mother's blindness was every bit as much my doing as the goblin's.

"Stop it, Cassie," Diana said, her voice as hard and cold as glacial ice. "Focus."

I dug my nails into my palms, and then knew my spells again. I didn't know what to cast first. The spell to protect myself wouldn't extend to the others. Even if Diana cast her own protection, it would leave Mother exposed.

"Stupid girl," the goblin said to me. "Did you think the pitiful magic you learned from the finder woman could stop me? A finder of lost things, but no talent beyond that most simple magic. How could she teach you anything to hurt me? I have lived a thousand years, faced magic stronger than you can even dream of, and still I stand here before you. You know nothing, Mage. And for your arrogance, you will suffer."

My throat went dry. My knees threatened to buckle. And somehow, I laughed.

"I've already bested you once, Gremhahn," I said. "You know I can do it again."

It was the goblin's turn to laugh. "Tell yourself that, but you know the lie of it. You know that without your seal friends you would have drowned. Where are those seals now? I don't see them."

I swallowed hard. The gremhahn was right; he would have won had the seal not saved me. But his gloating might be turned to my advantage if I could enchant him while he was too busy being proud of himself to stop me.

As he opened his mouth to say more, I cast a quick, two-word freezing spell, stopping him before his words escaped. For a long moment only the gentle sound of the ocean broke the silence.

"What's happening?" Mother said.

Diana said, "Cassie froze him."

Mother turned her head in the direction she'd last heard my voice. "Good for you, Cassie. Now, we must end the curse on you and then get Jimmy back."

"And the curse on you," I said, my voice breaking. If we did the curse-breaking spell, would Mother's sight return? The only way to know was to try it. I couldn't bear to think it might not work.

"If I unfreeze him," I said, "are we ready?"

We'd practiced this spell repeatedly together. I'd practiced it alone as well, and thought Mother and Diana likely had, too. Both women nodded. Diana was already holding Mother's hand. I moved to Mother's other side and took her free hand.

"On the count of three," I said. "One."

We had to be fast.

"Two."

We couldn't give the goblin time to throw out a counter spell.

"Three."

I freed the goblin from his frozen state and began the chant. A moment later, Diana joined with her part—different words that she said around mine, so that the chant began to sound like a song. When Mother joined with her part, we became a chorus, sometimes saying the same words but mostly not. Sometimes I was silent while Diana or Mother took a solo, but usually all three of us had a part. A sense of competence and rightness flowed through me—like being three different instruments in an orchestra, each playing individual melodies that melded into a single, much grander whole.

I kept my eyes on the sea goblin. His fingers were stuffed into his ears like a child. He'd tried that trick before. He wouldn't fool me a second time. We three raised our voices high.

The starfish at my throat warmed, grew hot. Energy poured through me. I was the flame and the fire, burning with the magnificent heat of magic. Nothing could stop the power we three had harnessed. Nothing save the gremhahn. Nothing would—

Mother squeezed my hand. I couldn't take a moment to glance at her, but didn't need to. She trusted me, believed in me. I raised my voice louder still. We together were the song, but I alone was the arrow that would pierce the goblin's black heart so that no other child would be torn from its family, no other parents would suffer the pain of having their child disappear in the night.

I turned Mother's hand loose. She and Diana continued chanting behind me, the trio turning to a duet as I strode toward the sea goblin. I didn't reach up to feel in my hair for the stars the goblin had put there—a way to know if his curse on me was broken. I no longer cared. Destroying the goblin was all that mattered.

I cast another cloaking spell as I walked so the goblin couldn't see me coming. It had to work in my favor. I didn't know a spell to destroy the gremhahn, had no idea what I'd do when I reached him, but I was the arrow launched by Diana's bow—I'd strike true.

Except—

Behind the gremhahn on the shore, another sea goblin appeared, emerging in the waves, wearing Dr. Gremhahn's face and clothing, and carrying his small black bag. My heart shuddered. Pax had said there was only one. How could another come from the ocean?

Not just one, but two, and three, and then four—emerging from the waves, walking through the surf as if they walked on dry land, waves breaking around them but having no effect.

And behind them, more Dr. Gremhahns emerged—a squadron of goblins approaching the surf line, heading toward me.

Panic sped my thoughts. Where had these goblins come from? How would I—or could I—deal with so many at once?

Mother and Diana continued their chanting behind me, with no change in tone or rhythm. For a moment I was grateful Mother couldn't see this army of goblins and be frightened by them. But Diana seemed blind to them as well. If she saw them, surely Diana would call out to me, give some advice, change the chant to help me with this new threat, cast some spell herself.

Nothing.

I was on my own.

Think, Cassie. Think. I didn't even know how to disarm and destroy one goblin—how was I going to manage dozens?

Something new appeared in the surf—a large harbor seal. The seal had its head out of the water and was looking straight at me. Looking at me and barking, as if trying to tell me something. Seals had helped me before, but there was only one gremhahn then. How could one seal stop more goblins than I could count?

The seal swam toward the last of the multiple Dr. Gremhahns—the only one still in the deeper surf. The seal dove under the water. The gremhahn suddenly jerked and disappeared beneath the waves.

One down, I thought. Dozens to go.

The seal broke through the water and rose into the air, leaping in a way I didn't know seals could, more like a dolphin or a whale, breaching out of the sea. And held in its mouth was the goblin, writhing. The seal threw the goblin high into the air. The gremhahn's arms and legs flailed. His doctor's bag fell and sank into the ocean.

Just as the goblin reached the apex of the throw, it burst into a geyser of black sparks that rose up and then fell onto the water and vanished. Unconsciously, I reached up and felt the stars in my hair. They were still there, as cold, hard, and solid as ever.

But . . . but, I realized, that shower of black sparks meant something. Most likely that the extra Dr. Gremhahns weren't real. The one, real goblin was still under my enchantment. How could he cast a spell to make me see goblins that weren't really there?

If his magic was stronger than mine . . .

Was the seal part of the trick, not really there, either—an illusion to make me believe I had an ally in hopes I'd relax my guard? If the seal were real, how could it drag down and then toss up an illusion? Were both illusions? What if my stars weren't real, either? Had we broken the gremhahn's curse on me, but he'd fooled me into believing the stars were still there? Was Mother truly blind or only enchanted?

I thought all of this in less than a breath. I had to make a choice—believe the other gremhahns were real and try to deal with them all at once, or one or two at a time, whatever I could manage—or believe there was only one. I chose to believe in one, even as the other goblins flowed onto the shore and rushed toward me like a swollen river, their mouths twisted into sneers, their eyes not Pacific blue like Dr. Gremhahn's, but as hard and black as obsidian blades.

Not real, I told myself, and turned my attention to what I hoped was the only real sea goblin. Something had to be done with him. Something fine and permanent. But what?

Please God, I muttered, *or gods and goddesses, forces of light, whatever's out there—help me now.*

Gibberish burst into my mind and words leaked out from between my lips, words I'd never heard before but felt had to be said. The words—a sentence really—were like a round, the first and last word the same, so that ending was also beginning again. On and on I repeated the stanza, the words circling around and around as I strode toward the one, true gremhahn, my voice growing louder the closer I came to him. I realized with a start that I did know some of the words —the dissolving spell to end the gremhahn's obsession with Mother and me was woven in with the gibberish.

The goblin was hopping from foot to foot, as though the sand had burst into flames beneath his feet. He'd hunched into himself, his hands clamped over his ears, while his many twins calmly shambled up the sand toward me.

What if I was reading that all wrong? What if that cramped posture was how he cast his spells? What did I know about the gremhahn? Nothing. Believing he acted and reacted like we did would was foolish.

The seal was still in the surf, watching.

You can help me, too, if you like, I thought toward the seal, while I kept on with the gibberish spell, still wondering what to do with the damn goblin.

The seal barked, then turned to look out to sea. My heart seemed to freeze mid-beat. A wave already as high as a two-story house was building and rushing toward the shore.

Tsunami.

I needed to warn the people on the beach, tell them to run. Except the water at the shore wasn't receding. Was the growing wall of water real or another illusion? I had no way of knowing as I watched the wave build higher and higher—twenty, twenty-five, thirty feet high, flinging itself toward the beach.

The many Dr. Gremhahns still advanced toward me with odd, shambling steps.

The giant wave grew higher and higher, rising up toward a bruise-colored sky and racing for the shore.

The seal lazily turned on its side and raised a flipper in the air. Surely ocean animals would know if danger approached.

More gibberish words slammed into my head. I stared at the wild water and recited the new words over and over. The roar of the towering wave howled in my ears. Flecks of foam and drops of water fell on my skin. I kept chanting even as the wall of water crashed over me. All the people up and down the beach would drown and it was my fault for not warning them. I was going to die. My Mother. Diana. But the sea goblin—the ocean was his home. He'd do just fine.

The wave poured over me, the cold, gritty water nearly

knocking me off my feet. I knew the inevitable moment when the water would begin to subside would come, sucking me and everyone on the sand into the sea. But I kept chanting. I'd cast whatever spell the gibberish words worked until my last breath.

The wave was still spilling over me when I felt it also begin to recede—a massive pull against my back. I braced my feet and hoped to finish the spell before the wave dragged me into the ocean to my death.

Water pounded my back and sluiced around my sides, but it didn't drag me. When the giant wave had receded, I stood on the beach, dry as old bones. Mother and Diana stood where I'd left them, no longer holding hands, no longer chanting, as still as stones.

Something was gone though, taken by the wave—the goblin's twins.

The gremhahn was still there. The one true goblin. He stood, hands on hips, a sneer on his face.

I touched my hair and felt a star, their wretched hardness yet another reminder of the sea goblin's power.

I'd wanted to break the curses on Mother and me. I'd wanted to make sure the goblin couldn't steal any more children. I'd failed on both scores—and Mother was blind. It would have been better if we'd never tried at all.

I raised my hand and started the protection spell, begging one more moment before he came for me, time enough to think, to know what to do next when I was all out of spells.

The starfish at my throat wriggled and squirmed against my skin as though fighting to free itself from the silver chain that held it. It grew warm and then hot, almost too hot to bear against my skin.

The gremhahn's sneer turned to a smile. He started to speak.

I smelled the acrid stench of burning flesh. My flesh, searing beneath the silver starfish.

The gremhahn's smile fell away. His hands flew up in front of his chest. A spell, I thought. He's preparing to enchant me and there's nothing I can do to stop it.

The heat at my throat was unbearable, I reached up to tear the starfish away from my throat. Before I could, a pulse of visible energy, silver and shimmering, flying straight as a ruler, burst from the starfish and struck the gremhahn in the middle of his chest.

The power of it shook me to my core. My knees trembled. I struggled to stay on my feet.

The goblin burst into flames. I could see him through the fire, screaming, his flesh melting like wax. The starfish sent out a beam of blue light that struck through the fire to the goblin. Sparks flew out of the fire, sparks as black as a starless sky, rising into the air as though from a campfire, spreading over the beach. Sparks that grew bigger and bigger and then—

Winked out.

EIGHTEEN

Hermosa Beach, California
July 10, 1924

*D*iana led Mother to where I stood. Mother slipped her arm over my shoulder and gave me a quick squeeze. I tried to smile, but couldn't quite manage it. My body and mind were exhausted. Every nerve felt singed. Even if I had forced a smile, Mother couldn't see it. There was no time to rest, not with one more task before me. I drew in a deep breath, straightened my spine and cast the calling spell for Jimmy.

The last word had barely left my lips when a harbor seal pup appeared just off shore and made its way toward the beach. My heart beat wildly. A year of waiting, searching, hoping, giving up and then hoping again, seeing and losing him that day on the beach—and here he was again. I quickly expanded the cloaking spell to include him, too. The pup barked. Mother started to run to him, but Diana held her back. I started the spell—pronouncing each word carefully, clearly—to free Jimmy from his seal form. Mother joined in, and then Diana—three needed to end a transferred curse.

The seal watched us and slowly blinked its dark brown eyes.

I huffed out a breath and looked to the sky. What had we done wrong?

I started the spell a second time, and again Mother and Diana joined in.

Again only a seal stood with us on the beach.

My jaw clenched. Determination flowed through my veins. I clutched the now cool silver starfish in my hand, closed my eyes, and started the spell a third time, my voice ringing loud above Diana's and Mother's.

Diana gasped, then laughed lightly. I opened my eyes, half afraid to look.

Jimmy stood on the beach.

Not my four-year-old brother, but Jimmy at his right age, five. He was naked without his sealskin, and he looked around, with fear and confusion clear on his face.

"He's back, Mother," I said. "Jimmy's back."

She let out a grateful sob and reached out blindly for her son, but he was too far away for her to touch.

Diana nudged me as she ran past, heading for Jimmy.

My brother didn't know her, but he seemed to slowly be recognizing Mother and me. He let Diana take his hand and lead him to us. Mother sank to her knees and wrapped her arms around her son.

∽

Jimmy had hardly spoken since he'd been restored to his human form. His body stayed as tense as a wire about to snap. All through the ride home, sitting on Mother's lap in the back seat, he'd been silent, his eyes wide, his head on a swivel as if trying to see everything at once.

His first smile crossed his lips as we pulled up to the house. We'd decided to go to Mother's rather than the beach house, even though it was closer, thinking Jimmy might feel safer and more comfortable in the place where he'd spent most of his life and away from the place from which the gremhahn had snatched him. When we walked into the house, Jimmy's little shoulders, which had ridden up around his ears on the ride, relaxed to a normal position. His small smile in the car opened to a wide grin.

"Are you hungry, Sweetie?" Mother asked him, feeling her way down the hall with her free hand as she led him inside.

He shook his head. "Tired," he said, and now his shoulders slumped and he fisted his eyes.

He was still wearing the towel we'd wrapped him in at the beach, and I realized there was nothing here in his new size except old clothes of mine. I found a pair of shorts that we pinned to fit his waist and one of Father's undershirts that hung down practically to his knees, and put him to bed.

"Tom-Tom," Jimmy said, reaching toward his old teddy bear, still waiting on the shelf since the day my brother had vanished. I got it for him, kissed his forehead, and slipped from the room. Mother stayed, and I heard her singing a lullaby.

Diana was tired, too—we all were. She said to tell Mother goodbye for her and headed out to catch the Red Car back home. I sat alone in the kitchen, fatigue weighing me down but adrenaline humming in my veins. I lit the wood in the stove and put on the kettle to make tea, adding enough water for each of us to have a cup. I rummaged in the icebox but didn't find anything I wanted to eat. I found a boysenberry pie in the pie safe and cut a big piece and ate it while I waited for the water to boil. I hadn't realized I was famished.

The teakettle had just begun to whistle when Mother—her arms out in front of her, feeling for walls—made her way back into the kitchen. I was glad she couldn't see my face screw up with pain as I watched her.

"He's sleeping," she said, walking cautiously to the table. She felt for a chair and collapsed into it.

I filled a tea ball with orange pekoe leaves, put it in Mother's favorite porcelain teapot, the one with a ring of violets around the fat pot's belly, and poured in the boiling water.

"Does he remember what happened?" I asked.

Mother shook her head. "I don't know. I don't think so, consciously, but unconsciously, he very well may. There's plenty of time to figure out what he remembers or doesn't in the coming days. For now, he needs to rest, to know he's home, and he's safe."

I nodded and yawned, then poured the tea into celadon green cups and gently guided Mother's hand to one.

"Do you want to stay the night?" she asked.

"Yes," I said, thinking I'd probably move back permanently, to help with Jimmy. Newly blind, Mother would have a hard time on her own. I reached up and fingered the stars in my hair. We'd destroyed the gremhahn, but hadn't won all that we'd fought for.

I'd settle for having my brother back. If I could find a way to cure Mother's eyes, I'd live with my stars and what they meant, and be happy.

A noise startled both Mother and me. We swung our gazes to the doorway. Jimmy stood there, his thumb in his mouth. He took it out and said, "The seal tell me something."

"What, Sweetie?" Mother said.

Jimmy kept his gaze locked on me. He drew in a deep breath and his hands formed loose fists, as if he were trying to remember the words exactly.

"One more blast of magic," he said. "Trust yourself."

A great cloud of energy seemed to burst inside me. The silver starfish at my throat warmed. In my mind's eye, I saw words written in silver script. Words I didn't know, had never seen before, and yet my mouth seemed to know exactly how to say them, as if I'd known them my whole life. Words that felt like music as I said them.

A sound like the tinkling of breaking glass whispered in my ears. I broke off the words—they seemed done now—and looked down. Tiny stars lay scattered on the kitchen floor. They glowed bright yellow for a moment and then flame red —and then were gone.

I cautiously ran my fingers through my hair. Nothing.

No stars.

I laughed once and swung my head to Mother.

"I saw them," she said, her voice thrilled. "I *saw* the stars fall."

You did?" I said. "You saw them with your eyes—not some sort of magic vision? You can see?"

Yes," Mother said. "Yes."

We broke into that mad laughter that is relief and joy combined.

Jimmy stared at us.

"Tired," he said. "Sleep now."

"My beautiful boy," Mother said, and crossed the room to sweep him up in her arms and put him back to bed.

When she came back, she sat at the table again and said, "You should go home."

"I'll stay," I said, though in truth, with Mother's sight back, I did want to sleep in my own house, my own bed, with my own things around. So much had happened today. I wanted time to think about it.

"Go home," she said.

"I'll come tomorrow or the next day, whichever you think is best for Jimmy. He'll have some adjustments to make."

Mother nodded and sipped her tea.

"Something you need to know, Cassie," she said.

I saw that Mother was rethinking what she'd planned to say—deciding if she wanted to say it or not. My stomach clenched.

"It's your young man," Mother said. "Diana told me what he is. He's not natural."

"What does that mean?" I said.

"He isn't who he seems to be."

"Mother," I said, exasperated and too tired for mysteries. Fear slithered through me. I remembered his kiss, how it made me feel. Was he playing me for a fool?

My insides froze with a terrible thought. "Is Pax a gremhahn disguise?"

"No," Mother said, and relief flowed through me. "But you'd best ask him who and what he really is. It's not my place to say. It should come from him."

I remembered the first day I took Pax to Diana's, the sour looks she gave him. But she'd seemed to warm to him later. If he were something horrible, she never would have done that.

I stood and kissed her cheek. "I'll talk to you tomorrow."

I slept most of the ride home, the gentle swaying of the Red Car lulling my sprung nerves and exhausted body. Jimmy was back. The curses were broken. We'd done it.

NINETEEN

Hermosa Beach, California
July 11, 1924

Scout snuffled in her sleep, her paws running in some dog dream, the motion rousing me from a dream of my own that vanished at waking.

I got up and looked in the mirror. How could I look the same as always after yesterday? It didn't seem right, but there I was, the same Cassie—minus the stars in my hair. I lifted the starfish necklace, wondering if it had burned me, leaving a scar. It should have, as hot as it had flared. It seemed something should mark me as changed, but there was no outward sign at all.

Scout jumped down from the bed and padded down the stairs.

"Are you hungry?" I said, following her. I was famished. I made breakfast for both of us: kibble for her; eggs, bacon, toast, and tea for me.

I thought about Pax while I ate. Pax, who was "unnatural," Mother had said. What did that mean? I finished eating and washed the dishes, still wondering what Mother and Diana knew that I didn't. I combed my starless hair, put on a cream-colored lace tea dress, and went to find out.

I spotted him coming down the Strand, dressed in white linen trousers and jacket, a light-blue shirt, and a straw boater. I saw three girls swivel their heads to watch him walk by, then turn to each other and whisper. He seemed immune to the numerous and lustful stares women sent his way. He was closer to the Berth Hotel than I was, and I worried he'd disappear inside before I could catch up. I sped my steps and caught his arm just as he turned to go inside. My stomach knotted while I wondered what to say, how to phrase the question, now that we were face to face.

Pax raised his eyebrows and peered at me. "You have something to ask me?"

I could never play poker. My face gave away my thoughts every time.

I nodded. "I do, but it's personal. Can we go somewhere private?"

"My room?"

I hesitated. A proper lady would never go alone into a gentleman's room. But I trusted Pax, no matter what Mother had said.

I followed him through the lobby and down a corridor to his large and bright room that held a bed, a small wardrobe, and a sitting area with two chairs. A large, full carpetbag, nearly big enough to hold a body, lay tucked to one side of the bed.

"What do you keep in there?" I said, looking at the bag.

"Is that what you came to ask me? Your primary question?"

"No," I said, "but I'd like to know."

"Ask your important question," he said, settling into one of the chairs and inviting me with a nod to take the other.

"The first may lead to the rest. I assume there is a rest. Likely a whole slew of them, once the gates are opened."

I remained standing. "What are you, Pax?"

He smiled slowly. "An odd question." He spread his hands wide. "What you see. Why do you ask?"

I sat in the second chair, smoothing my skirt with my hand. "The first day we went to Diana's, she kept looking at you funny. Then the two of you went into the kitchen and when you came out, she was all smiles and light."

"Perhaps I charmed her," he said.

I shook my head. "No. I think you told her something. And she told my mother. Mother says you aren't natural. She wouldn't say what she meant by that, only told me to ask you."

Pax regarded me a moment, then nodded. He stood and walked the few steps to the bed, picked up the bulging carpetbag as if it weighed nothing, and headed toward the door. He looked over his shoulder at me. "Come on. I'll show you."

We walked down to the shore, Pax leading the way with strong, sure steps. I shivered a little, remembering what had happened on the beach the day before.

He set down the bag and glanced toward a group of girls lazing on blankets nearby. "A cloaking spell would be good now."

My heart beat fast, wondering what he had to show me that needed cloaking. My curiosity had ramped up to nearly bursting level. I cast the spell and nodded at him to proceed.

"I think you've known for a while what I am, Cassie," he said, as he knelt and opened the bag.

I almost said the word, almost said *selkie*, but held my tongue.

He reached into the bag and drew out what looked like a large fur coat. He slipped on the fur, and instantly a large, beautiful harbor seal stood where Pax had been. The seal gave me a look and moved toward the water more gracefully than any seal I'd ever seen move on land. Moments later, he disappeared beneath the water. He reappeared, rolled onto his side, and slapped the water with his flipper—a pretty clear invitation to join him.

I took off my shoes, held the hem of my skirt in my hands, and waded into the water. SealPax swam up next to me, rolled onto his side again and splashed water my way. There were maybe ten or so other people in the water but they couldn't see us under the cloaking spell.

A thought struck me. "It was you who saved me when I fell into the sea, wasn't it? And you who brought the giant wave that washed away the false goblins."

The seal didn't answer, but sidled back onto the sand. I followed, wringing seawater from my wet skirt with my hands. The seal gave a shake and Pax stood in front of me again, the seal skin at his feet.

"You didn't think you wanted my help," he said, pushing some errant strands of wet hair away from his forehead, "but I believed you might need it."

He was right about that.

"Well, thank you."

"You're welcome," he said, and grinned.

I pursed my lips and hit his shoulder. "You could have told me. We talked about selkies. You even said you'd seen them, but made it sound like a joke."

He shrugged. "I could have told you, but I didn't want to."

There wasn't much to say to that. It dawned on me that the reason Pax couldn't help with breaking the spells was that he'd already planned to help in another way.

"What do you want to do now?" I said.

"Now I want to kiss you," Pax said, and did.

It was the same as the last kiss, a frizz of lightning

starting at my lips and spreading through my whole body—
and it was different. Deeper. We shared secrets now. He
knew I was a mage. I knew he was a selkie. The kiss sealed
our trust in the other.

He ran his fingers through my hair.

"Your stars are gone," he said.

"Yes," I said. "Jimmy delivered your message perfectly."

I guessed it was relief that brought the start of tears to
my eyes.

Pax let me have the moment, then gently wiped away the
tears that had spilled onto my cheeks.

"Walk?" he said lightly, as if it were the most normal and
natural next thing to do. The marine-layer clouds had
burned off and the sun shone brightly.

He took my hand and we headed down the beach, vaguely
toward the Palos Verdes hills, though getting to them was a
longer walk than I felt in the mood for just then.

I thought that tomorrow I'd ask Diana to teach me a
shape-shifting spell, one that would let me be a seal for a
while, to swim the wide ocean with Pax, in his home.

Tonight, there were other things to do.

ALSO BY ALEXES RAZEVICH

The Ahsenthe Cycle—Each book in *The Ahsenthe Cycle* deftly blends elements of science fiction and fantasy, satisfying those wanting something new. Readers looking for solid world building and strong female characters will especially enjoy this series.

BOOK ONE: *KHE*

BOOK TWO: *ASHES AND RAIN*

BOOK THREE: *BY THE SHINING SEA*

SHADOWLINE DRIFT – A PSYCHOLOGICAL THRILLER WITH SCIENCE FICTION AND FANTASY ELEMENTS, PERFECT FOR FANS OF INCEPTION AND LOST.

JUMPER: A SHORT STORY IN WHICH WORLD-CLASS SHOPPER, MADDIE BRESSLIN, ACCIDENTLY REMAKES THE WORLD. MAGIC REALISM AND A LITTLE STRANGE.

Coming in 2018: Supernatural mysteries featuring Cassie's great granddaughter, psychic Oona Goodlight, and Oona's wizard partner, Diego Adair.

If you'd like to be among the first to know when these books are available, I'd love it if you'd sign up for my VIP Readers at http://eepurl.com/08229.

ACKNOWLEDGMENTS

Many thanks to Meg Xuemei, Randy Jackson, Dan McNeil, Richard Casey, and Susan Marschner, wonderful writers all, for their help in shaping this story. Thanks also to the Hermosa Beach Historical Society, and especially to Chris Miller, for historical information. Anything I got right is due to them. Any mistakes are my own. Much gratitude to the lovely people who frequent my Facebook author page, especially those who helped name Pax and choose this cover. Y'all are the best. Thanks, as always, to Christina Frey, and to Doreen Martens for making this book better than I could on my own.

Much love to Larkin, Colin, and Chris Razevich—the three suns that light my world—and to Harley.

About the Author

Alexes Razevich writes speculative fiction of all sorts. She attended California State University San Francisco where she earned a degree in Creative Writing. After a successful career on the fringe of the electronics industry, including stints as Director of Marketing for a major trade show management company and as an editor for Electronic Engineering Times, she returned to her first love — fiction. She lives in Southern California with her husband. When she isn't writing, she can usually be found playing hockey or traveling somewhere she hasn't been before.

Twitter
https://twitter.com/lxsraz

Facebook
https://www.facebook.com/AlexesRazevichAuthor

News, Updates, Contests
VIP Readers

www.alexesrazevich.com/
LxsRaz@yahoo.com

Made in the USA
Middletown, DE
02 January 2018